A DARK DIARY NOVEL

GRAVE BURDEN

P. ANASTASIA

Grave Burden: A Dark Diary Novel
Copyright © 2020 by P. Anastasia

ISBN 978-0-9974485-9-7 (pb) Also in hc, audio, and ebook
Library of Congress Control Number: 2020901500

Other books by P. Anastasia:

Dark Diary (Paperback / Special Edition Hardcover)
ISBN 978-0-9862567-8-3 / 978-0-9974485-1-1

Exile of the Sky God
ISBN 978-0-9974485-8-0

Fates Aflame
ISBN 978-0-9974485-3-5

Fates Awoken
ISBN 978-0-9974485-5-9

Fluorescence: The Complete Tetralogy
ISBN 978-0-9862567-7-6

All rights reserved. Published by Jackal Moon Press
Lexington, Kentucky

www.JackalMoon.com

Special thanks to Thanomluk Art on Youtube

10 9 8 7 6 5 4 3 2 1

First Edition

Immortality is achieved by those we remember...

In loving memory of my dear friend, Ollie

1

KATHERA

I STILL had the ring.

Damn it. Why?

I had witnessed the brutal murder of the man who had given it to me. I had watched him suffer and bleed out, unable to stop a beast from tearing his ribcage apart.

I wanted to rid myself of the thing. I *should* have—but couldn't. I'd never even opened the black velvet box, never even acknowledged what I had meant to him.

Not that it mattered anymore; I had married another man—half beast, himself—who had done everything in his power to push me away for my own safety.

We were two old souls brought together by time, and we could not escape the chains by which we had been bound.

On the desk before me lay an old sketch I had done very early in my tattooing career. Between rigid, anxious lines of black ink resided a chapter of my life I could not erase.

And yet, I needed to.

I crumpled the drawing and tossed it into the trash. I *had* to forget everything that had happened between us. I had to let him go or the memories would destroy me.

In the beginning, my husband, Matthaya, had tried to explain to me how the curse would manifest in my veins, but I didn't understand him then.

The truth is, most emotions are dampened, while the sensations of hearing and vision are enhanced. At the same time, grief is amplified. Unable to combat such side effects, we are helpless to do anything other than harbor them. Whatever we died feeling remains with us forever, and we are haunted always by our final mortal regrets.

Matthaya was not without his own, but nearly four centuries have passed, and with me beside him now, he has begun to let them go. I, on the other hand, with the disease fresh in my blood, struggled to cope. All the things I had died thinking—the sorrow and fear that I had betrayed Derek's trust in me—left me hollow. He had taken me in when I had nowhere else to go, and he had tried to love me, even as my soul pined for another.

He was a casualty of my naive mistakes; I had never intended to hurt him.

There were footsteps outside my door, and I lifted my eyes toward the entryway. The door cracked open.

Matthaya entered and, almost immediately, gazed inquisitively toward the wastebasket. I hadn't yet learned how to conceal thoughts from my husband. As one-half of a bound pair of vampires, he could sense my feelings, and even read my thoughts, without really trying. Anything I dwelled upon raised a red flag—a glaring beacon in his mind.

His brow furrowed, but he tried to pretend he couldn't feel the pain roiling inside me. His racing thoughts prickled my brain, convincing me otherwise.

"How are you?" He came up beside me and cupped a hand on my shoulder. His other hand stroked the side of my neck and then his fingers coiled a lock of my hair.

"I'm fine."

He released my hair and pressed his other hand gently, but firmly, against my shoulder. "Are you sure? You can tell me anything, anything at all."

As a Sire, his natural ability to infiltrate my thoughts

allowed him to study me and to know me better than I knew myself. But he had promised early on not to pry into my secrets.

I wasn't ready to tell him the truth about the drawing I had just thrown away.

"Yes. I'll be fine," I replied, turning to look up at him and trying to smile. It was difficult to force the expression.

"All right." He forked his fingers through my hair and then leaned down to kiss the side of my neck, his fingertips sliding off my shoulder. "I'm here for you."

"I know."

He left the room and closed the door behind him, diligently dampening the click of the latch by slowly releasing the doorknob. I worked best when left alone—confined to my art studio and surrounded only by shadows and soft, flickering candlelight. My drawings came to me more readily this way. It was as though the act of being walled up and alone provoked my craft to come out of hiding.

Back when I had lived with my father and stepmother, I would often stay up late and design tattoos. I managed to squeeze in a few hours of rest, but for the most part, I was either too anxious or too afraid to sleep in the same house as my cruel stepmother.

Art calmed my nerves. It gave me a sense of control

and made me feel stronger.

Even with a lack of sleep, I had more energy back then. Now, every sketch was a battle between pen and paper. I knew I had them in me, but the ink didn't want to flow as freely as it had before.

Derek had taught me to do whatever it took to create—even if it meant boarding myself up in a tiny room and losing sleep. The end result would be worth it, he'd always tell me.

He had a strange way of thinking about art. He believed that true art could not be domesticated, and that its unpredictable, stubborn disposition gave it uniqueness and life.

Art would come when it was ready and, although you could coax it, you could never force it.

The tip of my black pen pressed down onto paper, and I began sketching the outline of an eye. I then darkened the lines of the almond shape with a thick black marker. The drawing—the one I had just thrown away—was the first tattoo that mattered in my career. It made me who I am today and molded me into the artist I will always be. It was the first tattoo I had inked on human skin. And it was the first tattoo I had done for *him*.

I drew a thin slit for a pupil and feathered the sides of the eye with decorative thorns, curling a pair of vines around the base as if it were an Egyptian motif. I was good at drawing eyes, so it was the first thing he had asked for after I applied for a full-time job at the shop.

In the beginning, I was an unpaid apprentice, but it was great experience. I helped around the shop with billing and cleaning, as well as shadowing Derek and other artists, and practicing on imitation skin. Once I turned eighteen, Derek offered to let me start tattooing clients, *if* I could nail a perfect tattoo for him first.

It was my "entrance exam," he had said. If I wanted to be a full-time artist in his shop, I needed to produce something he would be proud to flaunt.

The thought of it had made me nervous as hell, but it was a challenge I had accepted with as much grace as I could muster. The design took me days to finish, and I lost a lot of sleep over it. Derek loved dragons and old-school tribal patterns, so I came up with a tribal dragon's eye framed by two swirling, interconnected full-body dragons with wings embracing the eye on each side and tails tangled together at what would be the inner side of his bicep.

I remember the exact moment vividly:

"You ready for this?" Derek plopped down onto one of our padded chairs and rolled up his sleeve. I reached for a disposable razor so I could shave the area I was about to work on.

"If not, *you're* the one who's going to regret it," I said with a cheeky smile. I wiped down his arm with a paper towel moistened with disinfectant.

"True." He shrugged. "But I make a point to not regret any of my ink, so... it would have to be really, *really* bad for that to happen." He tapped me on the forearm. "I trust you, Kathera." He smiled warmly.

I reached for my carbon paper outline. "Do you want to see the finished design?"

"No. Like I said, I trust you. Besides, it's your career on the line, not mine." He smirked, trying to settle my nerves with humor.

I gently patted the template around his bicep, being careful not to rub it too much and smudge the design. I peeled off the carbon paper and fanned the area with my hand. The outline looked great. Part one: success.

The tattoo machine started to buzz.

I dipped the needles into black ink, took a deep breath, and then began putting down the outline of the dragon's eye.

That's when Derek pretended to flinch.

"Ouch!" he squeaked. I lifted the machine away from his arm.

My anxiety shot through the roof and I shrieked. "Derek, please!"

He seemed shocked at my reaction and his smile

went straight. "Yikes. Sorry."

"Please, stop screwing around," I said with a scoff. "I'm trying to concentrate."

"Just having some fun with you." He chuckled and looked the other way. "I apologize."

This wasn't Derek's first tattoo, that and he worked out—a lot. I think it was one of his hobbies outside of tattooing and fixing up his old Firebird. Certainly, my light-handed inking skills wouldn't cause him much, if any, pain. He was goofing around, trying to ease my nerves.

And it *sort* of helped.

The tattoo was going to take me at least a few hours to finish, so I needed to be as focused as possible. He had a high pain tolerance, so I could get it done in one sitting, and he'd made a point to not accept any more appointments that day.

We made good time on it.

I finished the outline in about an hour and a half and then we took a break before I started shading. A couple more hours went by before I had finally finished. I wiped off the remaining ink and then carefully applied a thin layer of tattoo balm to help with the healing process. It looked good to me. The lines were clean and smooth, and the color even. It looked *incredibly* good, actually, for my first REAL tattoo, and I was proud of it. Now, I just had to wait to see if it was good enough to get me hired.

"What do you think, Derek?" I asked, peeling off my gloves and tossing them into the trashcan. I gestured toward the mirror beside us. He stood and rolled his shoulder a few times, shaking out the stiffness.

He shot a quick glance at the mirror and then back at me, his dark brown eyes concealing his thoughts. "It's been a long day, Kathera. Why don't you go home and get some rest? We'll talk about it tomorrow."

My heart sank. *Tomorrow*?

What a way to get shot down.

I wanted to know right then and there exactly what he had thought of the work. I wanted to know how much he loved it... or hated it. I *needed* to know, and I wasn't going to get any sleep if I didn't.

But, he was the boss, so I shrugged and sighed, more loudly than I'd intended. "Okay." I slouched over in my chair.

He left the room and I started cleaning up.

The shop had closed for the night and the other artists had already gone home. It was just me and him.

As I was wiping down the chair, he called out from the other side of the office.

"Hey, Kathera, can I talk to you for a sec?" He gestured for me to come to the front desk.

I swallowed hard and walked over to where he was standing.

Oh, God... he must hate it.

I was scared. So scared that a lump formed in my throat and I couldn't swallow. So scared that my heart thumped like it was going to burst from my chest.

My life depended upon me getting the job. It was all I had been dreaming of for the past two and a half years. If Derek didn't want to hire me, I was screwed.

Art was my life. Tattoos were—

"We want to hire you," he said, beaming.

I exhaled. "Oh, my God, yes." I took a deep breath and sighed, grinning from ear to ear. "So you like it, then?" I crossed my palms over my heart as I tried to catch my breath.

"Yeah. Of course, I do." He smiled with his kind eyes, the dark browns and golds accentuating his grin. It wasn't the same gaze he'd set upon me the day I'd begun interning there. It was different. It was meaningful—proud.

A lot like his father, actually, may he rest in peace, who died later that year, not long after I had officially joined the team. It was sad for us both, because I knew him really well, even if some of it was only shadowing and asking questions. I'd been working with the shop in one way or another since I was fifteen. Derek's father was the closest thing I'd had to an uncle. He and Derek taught me everything I know today about tattooing and design.

"I talked it over with my dad the other day, actually," Derek continued. "You've been around here for a while and we appreciate your work ethic and your distinct style of art. You'll be an asset to this place. Fresh blood, you know?"

I nodded. My cheeks were hurting, but I kept on smiling.

"I needed to know that you wanted this job as much as my dad and I wanted to give it to you," he went on. "I knew that if your career depended on it, you'd put more work into designing a piece for me than anything else you've ever created." He gestured toward his bicep. "You did and I love it. You listened, and you designed something I can be proud to have forever. You've got tattoos in your blood, even if you don't have any on your skin." He winked. "Yet."

We both chuckled.

"Oh, and full disclosure, I may have snagged a quick peek at it before you even transferred the outline. I knew what I was in for, not that I had any doubts. Hell, you could have drawn a stick man and I would have hired you, all the same, because I know what you're capable of. It would have been the finest damn stick man anyone had ever seen!"

I laughed so hard, my eyes welled with tears.

Don't cry in front of your boss, idiot.

2

KATHERA

WHAT WOULD Derek think of me now? I had a tattoo—a wedding band illustrated and inked by my own hand. Matthaya shared the design. I drew inspiration from the Celtic dragon motif accenting his antique emerald ring. The pattern represented our origins, and I had inked them both on the eve of our wedding, an event I hope to never forget.

The ceremony took place at dusk, in a cozy vineyard just outside the city limits, surrounded by a warmly lit lavender garden, reserved just for us.

The sensation of our fingers entwined and the sight of candlelight glinting off Matthaya's waves of glossy black hair were memories I sought to embrace forever.

He squeezed my hand gently, and I was reminded of the human sensation of butterflies fluttering in my stomach.

I caught Matthaya's gaze lingering a moment on my bare shoulder before sweeping up my neck to meet my eyes. He smiled; a smile from him was uncommon, and for a split second, I felt the burden and guilt of my past lifting from me.

"You look incredible," he said, admiring the seafoam green, off-the-shoulder blouse with dark teal lacing I'd had custom-made for the occasion. Teal lace was a common accent for Irish brides in the old days, as was the sprig of white flowers tucked above my left ear.

I didn't know what to say, so I grinned, lips pressed together to hide my delicate fangs. As a recently converted vampire, I also had to stifle my bloodlust in the presence of the mortal priestess who had agreed to perform our marriage ceremony. The urges made me uneasy, and I tried to hide my discomfort.

Matthaya leaned closer. "It's okay," he whispered and then kissed the receptive skin behind my ear. I tilted my head and imagined what it would have been like to have lost my breath then.

"Kathera," Priestess Brenna addressed me.

It was time.

I lifted my face and looked the woman in the eye. She was pale as porcelain and dressed in deep royal-purple velvet with hints of charcoal-colored lace decorating her blouse and pleated skirt. "Will you accept Matthaya as your husband?"

My lips stretched a little wider as my fingers tightened around his. "Yes," I replied.

The priestess then turned to Matthaya, her lush, curly black locks sliding along her corset. "And do you, Matthaya, accept Kathera as your wife?"

I watched his stunning green eyes intently.

"Yes. Yes, I do."

Brenna turned gracefully toward the glass table at her side and lifted the lid of a wooden box. A subtle creak sounded and then she removed a long stretch of braided cords from inside.

"Remember, as your hands are fasted, these are not the ties that bind." She held the braided cords aloft. "Lift your hands," she instructed.

We did as we were told, our hands still clasped, and she continued.

"These are the hands that will passionately love and cherish you through your lifetime.

"These are the hands that will wipe the tears from

your eyes. Tears of sorrow and tears of joy.

"These are the hands that will comfort you in illness and hold you when grief torments your mind.

"These are the hands that will hold you and encourage you always to pursue your dreams.

"Together, everything you wish for can be found. Together, you will have peace and comfort."

The warmth in her voice touched my soul, each word like an embrace, soothing the tension in my veins. She brought the cords down below our hands and proceeded to loosely bind us together. Then she cupped her warm fingers atop ours and smiled earnestly. I sensed her sincerity all the way down to my bones—it was a talent I'd acquired with my transformation: hyperawareness of a human's true emotions.

"All things of the material world eventually return to Mother Earth," Priestess Brenna continued, "unlike the bond your spirits share, which is destined to remain. May you be forever as one. Passion and fire. Eternal and unyielding. You are now as your hearts have always known you to be—Husband and Wife." She stepped back and bowed her head to Matthaya, an earnest glimmer of joy sparkling in her hazel eyes. "You may kiss your bride."

Matthaya turned toward me. A wave of contentment coursed through him, and his peace of mind placated me. I flexed my fingers around his as he took one step closer and then kissed me.

℘ ℘

I put down my sketchbook and removed the braided silk wedding ties from a box near my desk. As I coiled them around my fingers, I closed my eyes and thought about the promises they represented. Becoming Matthaya's in heart, soul, and body had not been the difficult part. Becoming his in mind had. My racing thoughts taunted me always, reminding me of those whose deaths I'd caused, and I could not find silence in my own head. I could not find peace or freedom from the burdens of my past.

Derek's mother had come to my studio shortly after the incident, but she was left without real closure. Hiding such a deplorable secret from his family ate at me and I was crucified by my own regrets.

I wanted to tell Derek's mother the truth, but I couldn't. I couldn't tell her how my actions had made him vulnerable, and how my reckless pursuit of Matthaya had brought death herself—the hungry Sire, Ve'tani—straight to Derek's doorstep.

3

MATTHAYA

KATHERA HAD been acting unusual, but changes were to be expected. I didn't know how much of her personality would change after she had been taken, but I knew that a great deal of creative light had faded from her being. The lack of artistic energy sent her spiraling, once again, into a depressive state.

She was luckier than most vampires, as sunlight did not pose a hazard to her fair skin, but no dawn could distract her from the truth of what she had become. No sunrise would purify her from an eternal longing for blood.

I felt it continually—her mourning Derek's death. We are haunted always by our last regret, and as she had seen his blood pooling across the grass at her feet, that would remain branded in her memory.

I'd felt a great deal of her sorrow fade after I'd rescued her from her dive off the skyscraper months prior, but meeting Derek's mother had reopened the wound. Even now, I could sense Kathera in her studio, brooding over what never would have been—an ill-fated relationship with a mortal man—while threading our wedding ties between her fingers.

He had been kind to her, but she owed him nothing.

Derek had cared for her in her time of need, and she was not obligated to repay him. It was his decision to keep her, and to court her, and the truth of the matter was that she did not love him. Or, at the least, she had never intended to.

"Kathera?" I tapped on the door with the back of my hand and sensed her mind jolt with surprise. We'd grown very close, telepathically, but a handful of my actions slipped by unnoticed.

"Yes? Come in." She hadn't expected me to return so soon, but I had detected her growing hunger even before she had.

I pushed open the door. Candles burned in all four corners of her room, with several perched along the back of her desk. The satin ropes from our handfasting ceremony lay outstretched beside her, just as I had envisioned. White wax pooled precariously close to her sketchbook, ignored as she swept delicate, deliberate lines of ink across a page.

I stood behind her momentarily, watching as the drawing came to life—a wolf-like creature—something I had not seen from her before. Realistic animals were not her preferred subjects, but she was a master at conjuring incredible beasts of fantasy. Perhaps this would become one of them.

Strands of the wolf's mane came into view as she swiped her pen, rhythmically, like a precision machine replicating a design it had done a thousand times. Only she hadn't; this one was new. It didn't have the signature darkness in its eyes, for which her clients revered her. This wolf was placid. Domesticated.

"I brought this for you." I set a flute of liquid crimson on the table beside her arm. The glass clinked against the surface, but she didn't acknowledge it. "You... *should* drink something." She continued sketching in silence. "It's been... several days since—"

"It's horrible, isn't it?" She swerved around and looked me straight in the eye. "You think it's awful, don't you?" Before I could answer, she tore the page from its spiral binding and crumpled it in her hands.

"You're too hard on yourself," I said.

"No, I'm not." She tossed the paper ball into the waste-basket and turned to me. "I felt it in you." She shook her head. "You can't hide anything from me anymore." She pointed. "I felt you judging that work."

"I wasn't *judging* it." I knelt on one knee in front of her. "That piece looked as good as any of your others."

"What then?" Her eyes glittered with a fleeting blue spark of agitation. "What was it I sensed going through your mind as you looked over my shoulder? It wasn't a compliment, was it?"

I reached up a hand to cup her cheek, gazing into the sadness drifting through an ocean of rich azure.

"Well?" she prodded.

The answer wouldn't come quickly enough to my lips and she bolted up from her chair.

"You are depressed," I said, standing.

"How is that possible? I thought vampires couldn't fully experience human emotions."

"That is true, in part, but the grievances of your previous life cannot be erased. Our emotions may lie dormant, but that doesn't mean they've left us. You must learn to adapt." I grasped her forearms gently. She looked off to the side and clenched her jaw.

"Your work is beautiful, Kathera," I said. "And it always will be, as long as you learn to accept the limitations of what you have become. You can never return to what you once were."

Kathera's head turned and our eyes met again.

"This has happened before," I continued. "It is an ongoing struggle we will face for as long as we remain upon this earth. You are incredibly talented, and this world is fortunate to have you in it. As I am fortunate to have you in mine." I stretched an arm out to the table to grasp our wedding ropes. I brought one of her hands up to mine and entwined our fingers tightly. With my other hand, I coiled the threads around our wrists.

"These are the hands that will hold you and encourage you always to pursue your dreams," I whispered, squeezing her hand. "Even when they appear far from reach. Even when they seem impossible to find." Sapphire blue irises gazed back at me, the anxiety in them beginning to melt away.

There were days when nothing I could say or do could take away the painful memories piercing her soul, but every beast has a lullaby, and I knew exactly what hers was.

"Would you like to visit your mother tonight?"

She glanced at the shimmering ties around our hands and nodded slowly, a thankful, bittersweet smile tugging at her lips.

A moonlit walk in the crisp, fresh air would be good

for her, and the quiet company would bring her some peace.

Mothers have a way of doing that.

The tender breeze made Kathera's vivid burgundy hair dance around her face. I clasped my hands together in my lap and sat across from her on another bench, watching as she took in the calm surroundings of the cemetery. I would do whatever it took to quiet her mind. I had all the time in the world.

She stood and dead yellow and red leaves crunched beneath her shoes as she walked over and sat beside me. She reached for one of my hands, prying them apart so that she could drag one over to her lap and cup it lovingly. Her thumb brushed across my signet ring, tracing over the large emerald stone.

"I want to know who you are, Matthaya." She looked up at me. "Don't you? Don't you want to know what name your wife—*I*—might have assumed?"

Or what name Kathryn would have shared?

"You did not need to take my name to take my heart." My fingers squeezed hers.

"I know, but isn't there some part of you that wants to know who you were? Where you came from?"

"No." It wasn't a priority, but there had been times when it had crossed my mind.

"You're lying," she said, narrowing her eyes.

I couldn't hide much from her anymore.

"Perhaps. Yes. But I don't want to be haunted by my past—by the person I could have, or should have, been. It doesn't matter anymore. Does it?"

We had already agreed to assume the name I'd been using this century—Jackman. It was an uncomplicated surname with uncomplicated origins.

"It matters to me," she replied. "This is a beautiful ring and there are centuries of history buried within its facets, lurking behind these golden dragon engravings. But..." She released me. "I won't pursue it if you don't want me to. If you really don't care about who you are, then—"

"I care. If it concerns you, it concerns me."

4

KATHERA

A FAINT sensation tickled my shoulder and I twitched; fingers dragged toward my wrist until they brushed my palm and then grasped my hand. I flexed in response. My eyelids fluttered open, and it took me a moment to focus.

"Derek?"

A sweet smile curled his lips. "Good morning, beautiful." He was sitting on the edge of my bed.

I released his hand and sat up groggily, squinting from the bright golden light peeking through the blinds.

"What is it?" I asked. We'd been living together for a

little while, but he'd never woken me up quite like this before.

"I came to ask you what you wanted for breakfast." He shrugged and let out a nervous chuckle. "And... I've got to confess, you're really pretty when you're sleeping."

I didn't know how to respond to that, so I tugged my sheets up to my neck and lowered my face to hide my embarrassment.

"Derek," I muttered. "Don't get creepy, okay?"

"Sorry," he replied with a hearty laugh. "I'm just teasing."

He had a beautiful smile. It was bright, honest, and comforting. You could tell it was genuine by the way his eyes narrowed warmly. It was contagious, too.

He reached toward me and his warm hand cupped my cheek. Sunlight shimmered across his brown eyes.

"I love you, Kathera," he said in a voice that was nearly a whisper. "You know that, don't you?"

Yes...

All I did was nod slightly, my cheek brushing against his palm.

"And you know that I would do anything for you—anything at all?"

Again, I nodded.

He leaned forward and kissed me.

I couldn't help but close my eyes as his warm hands

held me steadfast. He felt so wonderful.

After our lips parted, he took a deep breath and sighed heavily.

He looked down.

Derek wasn't one to bite his tongue when it came to his feelings, and although I often appreciated his bluntness, sometimes it got a little too intense for me.

"It's hard, you know?" he started, scooting closer. "I'm not asking you to do anything you're not comfortable with, but I need to get this off my back."

I pulled my pillow up and tucked it behind me so I could rest my weight against it. "Sure. Go ahead."

"I love you," he said, trying to fight back the sadness wavering on his face. "I'm not going to lie. There have been times when I wished you'd reconsider our boundaries. I know it's important to you to wait until you're married, and I am trying very hard to respect your decision. But that doesn't mean it's easy for me." He reached out a hand to sweep his fingers ever so gently across the side of my neck. "I'd do anything for you, Kathera, and I'm not trying to ask for anything in return. It's just—"

"It's hard for me, too, sometimes," I uttered beneath my breath, ashamed, but hoping my honesty might soothe some of his pain. There were moments when the throes of passion consumed me. My body wanted him as much as he had wanted me, but I was better than him at hiding that.

Only a *little* better.

He traced a line across my collarbone. "You have beautiful skin," he said, fixated on the lace trim of my tank top. A moment later, his hand slipped off me, and his line of sight shifted to something across the room.

The silence was heavy and awkward.

I opened my mouth to reply.

Apologize, maybe?

I didn't know what words would make things better, if any.

He stood and shrugged off his discomfort. "I came to ask you what you wanted for breakfast," he said again, forcing a smile.

∎ ∏

Too many times I had thought back on our interactions, wondering if I'd made the right choices, or if my archaic desire to save myself before marriage had been nothing but torture to the man who had saved me from a spiral of depression. God knows what I might have done to myself had Derek not been there when Matthaya had walked out of my life for what I thought would be forever.

What would have happened to me had Derek not taken me in? He provided shelter and companionship in return for nothing but, perhaps, the hope that I would let him into my heart one day.

Remnants of my mortal past haunted me, so I tried to sleep them away.

But it didn't shut out the bad memories or dangerous thoughts. It didn't block the pain or stop my heart from aching with regret.

It only made things worse.

Unlike Matthaya, who ceased to dream at all anymore, I continued to have vivid, lifelike dreams. My mind became as active at rest as it was while awake. Before, I had been plagued by nightmarish visions of death and drowning, but now, a new and very different dream, formed of twisted realities, taunted me as I slept...

଼ ଅ

"I want to wait," I said, clasping onto my bare arms to brush away the chill and goose bumps. "I already told you this. I'm sorry I keep giving you the wrong idea. Maybe we should take some time off. Maybe—"

"I know that you're afraid of commitment," Derek replied, "and—especially—of making the wrong choice with the wrong guy." He moved closer and forked his fingers through my hair. "I understand how important that is to you."

I started trembling.

"In the beginning, I was fine with it," he continued, "but we've been together for months, and there's so much damn tension between us now. I'm not afraid to commit to you. I hope I've made that evident. But I don't know how else to prove just how committed I am. If you want me to back off and give you space, then I will, but it's going to put a hell of a strain on this relationship."

"I know." I fought back tears and tried to quiet my shuddering breaths. "I'm sorry for treating you this way. I didn't think it would be this hard."

"I love you more than I ever imagined it was possible to love someone, Kathera," Derek said, reaching for my hand. "There's nothing I wouldn't do to make you happy. Right now, everything inside me longs for you. And that's the problem. I need you so much, that it hurts to be around you anymore. You've come to me in the middle of the night and asked to stay with me, and I've obliged, pushing back expectations and..." he swallowed hard, "*desires*... out of respect for you. Because you're not like other girls. You wouldn't hurt me like... like *she* did."

His last serious relationship had landed him in the emergency room with critical injuries. Not only had the woman cheated on him, she had also started a rumor that Derek had abused her. It was a disgusting way to try to sever ties and make excuses for her infidelity. Those rumors eventually led to a violent physical altercation with one of her other lovers, which left Derek scarred for life and unable to trust women the same way.

"I've been patient," he continued, "but it's becoming unbearable. You let me so close, and then you push me away. The signals are all mixed, and I don't know what your boundaries are anymore."

The subtle lamplight glistened off his eyes as he stared into mine.

I took a deep breath and wiped my cheeks with my palms.

The sorry truth was that I enjoyed being close to him; I liked it when he caressed me with hands that longed for me, and when he kissed me in a way that made me believe I was the only woman he'd ever wanted. I savored the swirl of emotions that coursed through me when he held me tightly.

That didn't mean I was ready to sleep with him.

"I know. I'm sorry for how I've been treating you. The truth is..." I sniffled and looked down at my hands as I tangled them in my lap. "I'm conflicted, too. I thought I wanted to save myself until marriage, but when I'm with you, I can't think straight and..." I sighed.

"Trust me." He put his hand out to stroke my cheek. "I'll do my best to make sure you don't have any regrets."

I closed my eyes for a moment and took in a deep breath, appreciating those warm fingers against my skin.

I *did* trust him. If I hadn't, I wouldn't have come to him in the middle of the night that first time, seeking comfort when anxiety and fear wracked my brain.

Maybe I did love him.

Maybe I didn't know what love was, or I had a distorted view of what it should be.

It *was* nice to be there beside him, his gentle touch against my neck.

He felt so good, and his embrace was so warm. I felt safe. And whole.

I opened my eyes again and focused on his. He smiled sweetly and rested his hand on my bare shoulder, his fingertips massaging my skin.

Maybe I was overthinking everything.

"I do trust you, Derek." I reached out to graze my fingers across the side of his face; the stubble along his jawline tickled my fingertips. "I do."

His gaze drifted down to my lips, and then I let him sweep me up into a passionate kiss.

Every spark of his energy was focused on me, as if he had intended to win me over with that kiss.

And maybe he did... as my body began to tingle, and a sense of perfect harmony and contentment washed over me.

His strong arms embraced me and his tongue tasted mine, seducing me with his skilled, perfected craft. He knew exactly what I liked, and his intense hunger for me made me lightheaded.

He pressed forward, supporting me from behind as he lowered me onto my back against the plush comforter. Then he came over me, pinning my body firmly against the bed.

His hot breath swept against my throat as one of his hands inched up under my shirt to caress my ribs. My lungs quivered when he pressed a kiss against the hollow of my throat. Then the fingers of his other hand entwined with mine, and he pushed my arm over my head, against the mattress.

Every sensually warm, sex-starved curve of his body had brushed up against me in just the right way that it had me trembling involuntarily, my heart racing as my fingers tightened on his hips.

It felt good—the touch of his skin against mine, and the primal longings inside which implored me to let go of my inhibitions. He was a man in love wanting nothing more than to consummate his feelings for the woman he had chosen.

And there I was, unable to decide what I wanted.

My body wanted him, but my conscience...

He peeled his shirt up over his head, tossed it off the

bed, and then shifted to slide a knee between mine. He lowered himself back down on top of me and began folding my shirt up toward my breasts, planting a line of kisses across my stomach as my back arched. A playful pinch of his teeth against my side made me writhe.

I'd succumbed to his desire and absorbed it like a drug. My mind grew fuzzy and disoriented, but the decision became clear—I wanted more and I could think of nothing else.

Desire and triumph glinted in his eyes, as if he knew he'd finally gotten me where he had wanted me, and that there was no turning back.

His body pressed against mine and he brought his lips close to my ear.

I dropped my head back and gasped, my fingers inching past his neck and nestling into his short hair.

"I *will* marry you, Kathera," he whispered, the deep, visceral truth of his words forcing the last threads of reason from my mind.

∝　∞

I awoke, with a start, to the vibrant green of Matthaya's widened eyes staring down at me.

"What was that?" he asked, searching my face for

the answer. The moonlight reflected off his pale bare shoulders as he leaned over me.

"Only a dream," I replied, hoping he wouldn't pry the truth from my mind.

"Oh?" Matthaya knew me too well. "*Only* a dream? Somehow, I feel there was more to it than that." He moved beside me and leaned back against the headboard. "Do you want to talk about it?"

I sat up, too.

"When I was with Derek, I-I..." The words tangled upon my tongue. "He wanted... He'd hoped that I'd..."

"That's natural," he interrupted, confirming he already knew what I was stumbling over. "He was a man in love, and that is how we often think. When instinct takes over, we are driven by forces much more influential than mere reason."

"But, I said no," I added. "I told him that I wouldn't—not until I was married. I didn't want to sleep with him until I knew for sure he was the one I'd stay with."

"I understand." Matthaya's gaze drifted down to the tattoo across my finger and he stroked his hand over mine. "I love you, Kathera. You can tell me anything. No matter what it is or who it was with." His fingers wrapped around mine. "Please, don't hesitate to speak the truth. I have no right to be jealous of things you did, or even *thought* about doing, in my absence." His face tipped to the side and his eyes implored me to confide in them. "Was that dream a memory of something that had actually happened... or?"

"Well, I..."

Damn it. The words just wouldn't come.

But he waited, not an inkling of impatience about him.

"*Some* of the things in that dream *did* happen, but, in reality, I stood my ground and I said no. In my dream, I gave in." I felt relieved to have finally gotten the guilt off my chest.

The expression of sympathy on Matthaya's face didn't seem to change, but I noticed his lips fighting back a brief grimace.

"It's natural for you to question your past actions," he replied quietly. "To believe he deserved more of you than you had allowed him to have at that time. Your grief is making you overanalyze your choices in an effort to reconcile with the past. You feel that his death was caused by your decisions, but—"

"It was," I said flatly.

"You cannot spend eternity dwelling on it." His fingers released mine. "You simply can *not.*" The spice of anger tainting his words jarred me, and I sensed the remorse he still harbored over the unnecessary fatality Derek had become. "You made the decision that was right for you at the time, and—despite how his life may have ended—you owe him no debt."

5

KATHERA

"I'M GLAD the hurricane changed course, aren't you?" my client said, pushing back against the seat as she scrolled through social media on her phone. She kept her leg surprisingly still, in spite of her constant fidgeting.

I traced the dragon egg outline on the side of her calf with black. The machine's buzzing was more apparent than usual, and it rattled through my brain, putting me on edge.

Before I could answer her question, she changed the subject and said, "I still can't believe you don't have an online profile for this place. I'm surprised I found out about you, but I am so glad that I did."

I wiped off the excess black, then switched out the needles and began inking some texture details with pine green.

"But, whatever," she continued. "More time for me, I guess. I'm on fall break right now. A friend recommended you. She got inked about a year and a half ago. It was, like, a broken heart or something. Her breakup was tragic, but the guy was a dick, anyway."

I remembered that client. She was full of bitterness and sorrow, and I had wondered, at the time, if she might regret the tattoo.

She glanced down toward her calf. "Dragons are cool, though. So, were you a GoT fan?"

I lifted the needle from her skin as I looked up. "No. Not really."

"What? No way." Her brow furrowed. "I think you're the only person I've met who wasn't."

I was familiar with the series, but not interested.

She shrugged. "Oh, well. R.I.P., Jonerys."

I went back to coloring in the scales of the dragon egg. The *Game of Thrones*-inspired design began circulating several years ago, but I hadn't been asked to tattoo one before.

Mainstream images were not my preference, but with my creative energy fizzling, it made sense to work on something—anything—instead of letting my skills decay.

"I apologize for being quiet," I said, highlighting one of the shield-shaped scales with golden yellow.

"Huh?" She looked up from her phone screen.

I smiled and went back to work. She went back to scrolling.

I spent the next hour silently coloring and shading each scale, adding highlights and texture until the egg was complete. Behind my polished, intricate cover-up tattoo, was a poorly drawn, stick-and-poke "tattoo" of a baby dragon. It was tasteless and juvenile, like something out of a kid's coloring book, but less refined. Stick-and-poke isn't something to be disrespected, and many artists are wholly capable of producing beautiful, unique artwork with the right techniques, but this was not an example of that.

At least she could show off the dragon egg with pride. It had turned out quite lovely, even though it wasn't my design. It had hints of my style buried in the line-work, but the originality ended there.

"All done," I said, peeling off my gloves and tossing them into the trash. I'd just added healing balm and then a bandage.

"Thank you," she replied. "It looks friggin' amazing. So much better than that scratcher's crap. I shouldn't have let him practice on me." She rolled her eyes. "So stupid. Anyway, I appreciate it."

"You're welcome."

I walked with her to the front desk, where my new receptionist—a young man named Kieran—took care of the rest. Then my client and I parted ways. Like most fall break customers, I'd probably never see her again.

Matthaya had told me to stop working with them if I wanted to challenge myself, but I didn't want a challenge right now. I was struggling to rekindle my passion.

I didn't want to stay home and do nothing.

It was the middle of the day and the sun wouldn't set for a few hours. Matthaya stayed home, as he typically did, until dusk. It would get darker and cloudier as winter drew nearer, but until then, he'd stay away most of the afternoon.

This is also why I had agreed to hire a receptionist. It was, surprisingly, Matthaya's suggestion. Kieran was in his twenties and had medium-length, emo black hair with an electric blue streak over his brow; he considered himself a social outcast, but fit in perfectly with us. His hidden compassion and ability to listen and follow directions were traits I appreciated. He didn't ask questions about our odd hours, or odder complexions, and he did his job right the first time. I could feel that he was happy to have stable work with people who treated him like a human being and not a number.

Having him around the shop allowed me to stop worrying about all the little things, like booking appointments and consultations, and let me concentrate on my canvases and their design needs.

I *only* took clients by appointment, so anyone who walked in off the street had to go through Kieran first, and it saved me precious time.

"You've got one more scheduled for tonight," Kieran said.

I had just begun sanitizing the studio and packing up my autoclave bags when an itchy feeling washed over my skin.

"Kathera?" Kieran called, this time poking his head around the corner from the front desk to peer into my studio.

"I-I heard." I grimaced and clenched my teeth, trying to shake the uncomfortable twinge quaking through my veins.

Hunger.

Now is not the time.

I'd not yet learned how to predict or repress it, even though Matthaya was trying to teach me to be aware of the signs.

It would come at strange times. In weird places. Weird hours of day or night.

I'd be fine, and then suddenly all my skin would be crawling and a sensation of pressure in my ears would build. Then the sounds around me would grow louder—more intricate and disruptive.

With Kieran around and another client scheduled to come in soon, it was in my best interest to go home early. Else, I'd risk letting the hunger overwhelm me and... bad things could happen.

We didn't keep blood in the shop for *obvious* reasons.

"Actually," I started, sealing the last package and setting it onto a metal tray. "Would you mind rescheduling that one? I'm not feeling well. I think I should call it a day."

"Oh, sure, leave me with the dirty work," Kieran said with a laugh. "Clients love rescheduling."

I glared at him, more harshly than I had meant to; it was the hunger and anxiety setting in.

"But that's what you pay me for," he added nervously and then zipped back to his computer to look up the client's phone number. "I hope you feel better."

"Thanks."

I packed up my things and left the shop.

The tingling, itchy sensations intensified as I walked, and I fought to stay focused. We didn't live far, and I'd be home soon enough.

Assuming the hunger would subside. The thunderous rustling of the wind through the dying leaves made me flinch, the sharp crackling sounds grinding through my brain like twigs being snapped by my ears.

I heard voices in the distance.

I blinked several times in an attempt to reduce the colorful fringing beginning to take shape on my surroundings—indicators of movement and heat designed to assist us on the hunt.

This had happened before, and I'd been able to keep the symptoms to a minimum until I'd arrived home, but these were much stronger than they had been in the past.

The sheer intensity provoked me to take a different path, a shortcut, crossing through the cemetery instead of going around it. There were fewer people there, and I could take a brief break to try to calm the urges.

I found my mother's grave and sat beside it to rest.

Slowing down and closing my eyes helped dampen the primal impulses.

Matthaya had taught me this in the beginning. He'd taught me that whenever the hunger struck, I had to find a quiet place to rest and allow it to pass.

I was at peace near my mother's grave, tamed by pleasant memories of a life that once was.

It was also where I had met Matthaya. Before things grew complicated, we would sit and talk beneath the light of the moon.

I sat on the bench near my mother's tombstone and rested my hands in my lap, lifting my face up and taking in a long, deliberate breath of early autumn air.

Trees. Grass. Flowers that had been set upon the graves of others. Scents of those who had come and gone throughout the day—the fragrant perfumes and soaps they'd used to wash their bodies and clothes. All these things lingered in the wind.

I kept my eyes closed and let my mind drift off into a calm, meditative state, willing the approaching sunset to quell the hunger pangs.

And it did... eventually.

Darkness came like a thief, spiriting the sun away beneath a cloak of stars.

The wind blew, tousling my hair around my face, forcing me to tuck unruly locks behind my ears.

I sniffed the air. Humidity was high and the pressure changing.

It would rain soon; I felt it in my bones.

I pushed up from the concrete bench and turned to head home.

A familiar scent wafted by, causing me to freeze where I stood. It was a warm, vibrant amalgam of musk and amber, and it was familiar. Too familiar.

A twinge of discomfort flushed through my blood-stream and my adrenaline spiked, altering my vision to better detect movement in my surroundings.

I was not alone in the cemetery.

I swerved to confront the intruder and growled fiercely, baring my fangs.

"Hi," he said, raising an eyebrow while grinning fearlessly.

He was tall, broad-shouldered, and muscular. His skin had an unnatural tinge of yellow to it, the result of a fading olive tan. Ruddy bleach-blonde flecked his short dark hair, and his deep brown eyes had a hint of supernatural golden light circling the irises.

"Derek!?" I stiffened. "This can't be," I whispered, though neither my nose nor my eyes deceived me. "You died."

His presence launched my senses into overdrive, and a dozen colored outlines traced his silhouette, shifting in and out of focus as if he were a threat.

I'd watched him die.

He stepped closer to me. "Actually, I've been informed that the dead can't be taken." He smiled maliciously, so I could see his shiny new vampire incisors. "A Sire can't take someone who's already dead, because there has to be some life left to convert."

But, Ve'tani had torn him open... I saw him bleeding out. He was...

My chest tightened at the sickening revelation racing through my brain.

He was never dead?

We... I left him there... alive!?

Derek stretched out a hand toward me, but I quickly withdrew from his reach.

"You never pulled away from me before," he said with a scowl. His voice had an eerie timbre to it, reminiscent of the vile maker, Ve'tani.

Thoughts darted through my brain at breakneck speed, and confusion shrouded my mind as an overwhelming sense of guilt crashed over me.

It was *really* him.

I stood my ground and tried to stifle the hyperactive instincts so that my sight, and my racing thoughts, would stabilize.

He approached again and reached for me a second time.

Maybe I should have been leery, but my condition made me less cautious than my former self. I let Derek take my left hand into his, and I watched as he examined the band across my ring finger.

"This is new," he said, caressing the wedding tattoo with his thumb. "So... what should I call you? Mrs.?"

I was tempted to yank my hand away. Knowing that he was alive (in some sense of the word) planted a myriad of paralyzing thoughts in my mind.

Should I say something, or apologize, even? I wanted to.

Should I flee?

Why would I fear him now when I hadn't before?

My mind caught in a vicious loop of questions, not a single word came from my lips.

"I'm just curious," he added with a nonchalant shrug. "I'd like to know who ended up taking my place."

"No one took your place," I said, gazing into his dark brown eyes. They'd become unnaturally vibrant, flaunting bright golden undertones and a glimmer of bioluminescent light. "I thought you were dead. You were bleeding everywhere after th-that monster—"

"That *monster* saved my life," he hissed, squeezing my fingers. "After you and that bastard left me to rot in my own backyard."

"It was a mistake. I'm sorry for what happened to you," I said, making a feeble attempt to pull my hand away. "We didn't know."

"Are you sure *he* didn't know?"

No... But, he wouldn't have...

Would he?

No!

I trusted Matthaya.

"He wouldn't lie to me," I replied. My voice wavered. "Why would you suggest such a thing?"

"If you say so," he replied, turning my hand over to caress my palm in a circular motion with his thumb. "Have you missed me?"

His hand slipped down to my wrist and clutched me tightly. An intense urge to distance myself from him electrified me.

"It must have been hard going on without me," he said with a raspy voice. His vivid eyes fixated on mine as he lifted my hand.

I tried to pull free again, but my body felt heavy and slow, difficult to move, as if time had come to a crawl. In my mind, I thought to escape his grasp, but in reality, I hadn't moved an inch.

Derek jerked me forward and sank his fangs into the skin of my upturned wrist.

A searing burn jolted through me and my vision faded to black. A twisting, ripping sensation spiraled into each nerve, making me convulse.

Then I gasped, the air knocked from my lungs by the sheer force of him slamming my body against a wall that had appeared from out of nowhere.

I could see again, but things were different.

It was bright. Artificial light stung my eyes.

Everything was blurry, but I knew we weren't in the cemetery anymore.

Derek planted both hands near the sides of my head, pinning me against the phantom wall. As he leaned in closer, his hot breath against my throat made the hairs on the back of my neck perk up and goose bumps rise along my arms.

His body felt warm—something vampires are not.

The air became uncomfortably stuffy and my head started to spin as his fingertips crept across my collarbone.

"Don't fight it, Kathera," he whispered as his lips dragged up my cheek toward my ear.

Why can't I get away? I was frozen, unable to move.

A great hunger roiled inside him and it was as if he had opened up his mind so that I might witness his lust for me simmering there.

He wanted all of me, and he further established his intentions by wrapping his hands around the jut of my hipbones and forcing my body to be flush with his.

I groaned reluctantly and turned my face to the side.

"You wanted to give in before, didn't you?" he asked and kissed me behind my ear. "I felt it in you." A hand slipped up under my shirt. "You wanted me, but you wanted to wait." His fingers walked up my ribs. "Wait for... what was it again?"

He knew damn well the answer to that question. "Well?"

My lips quivered. I was so weak, I trembled. The room was closing in on me, and the only thing I could hear was his voice—his desperate, angry words, taunting me.

"Matthaya!" I tried to cry out, but it wouldn't manifest from my lips.

"No," Derek corrected, sneering in disagreement and shaking his head. "No. I don't think that was it." He kissed the base of my neck and slid his tongue up to my throat. "Ah. I remember." He took a deep breath and exhaled on my skin. "You wanted to wait until you were married."

I drew in a heaving breath and then coughed. My throat was so dry, I could hardly breathe. Sweat beaded on my forehead and I felt smothered.

Everything I was experiencing was human, but how?

The hand on my hip released me and latched onto my wrist, pressing my arm up and back against the wall. My legs shook, my knees were about to give out, and my heart ached more with every inch of my body he touched against my will.

"Well," he exhaled into my ear, "I think it's safe to say that you're married *now*."

He let go, and I plummeted to my knees. I used every

last ounce of strength to call out to Matthaya again.

Derek loomed over me. I crumpled over in a frantic attempt to put pressure on the oozing puncture wounds on my wrist.

Our surroundings went dark again and the night sky reappeared overhead, the illusionary walls and lighting fading away. I looked up, my gaze meeting the moon, wishing it would take the pain away.

Dark burgundy blood trickled down my fingers and I could barely keep my head up.

"Get away from her!" Matthaya's voice resonated from nearby. I lifted my face toward the sound but could only see fractals of light and distorted shapes.

"Matthaya?" I muttered. Cold fingers grasped my shoulder and Matthaya's presence grew as he knelt beside me.

"Are you all right?" His words were like echoes, bouncing through endless space.

"For now," I uttered.

He released me and stood. "What did you do to her?"

"This isn't high school," Derek replied, chuckling. "If you don't know, I suggest you ask her."

A deep, animalistic growl rumbled in Matthaya's throat as he reached for my wrist and turned it over. The growl intensified and he let out a loud, beastly snarl toward

Derek. "You... you bit her? You twisted bastard!"

Derek laughed callously. "Hey, some girls like that kind of thing."

Matthaya roared and the earth quaked beneath me.

"Not that *you* would know anything about what women want," Derek continued. "You broke her heart, vanished into thin air, and then later came skulking out of the shadows to try to win her back, only to destroy *my* life in the blink of an eye. You hurt Kathera, and then you stole her from me, leaving your Sire, Ve'tani, all alone in the darkness. You call *me* a 'twisted bastard,' but you treat women like shit."

The tremors rippling through my body slowed and I tried to stand, staggering to catch my balance. Matthaya noticed and helped pull me to my feet. My vision had finally returned to normal, and I gazed down at the festering puncture holes in my wrist. Blood continued to escape, so I brought it close to my face and licked it quickly.

The reaction between saliva and my open wound caused the blood to bubble up, sizzle, and burn. The throbbing sensation made me cower as the skin began to seal itself closed and the holes began to fade.

Matthaya clenched a fist. "You'll pay for this!"

Derek had already begun to back away from us. "Oh, I know," he replied with a snarky nod. "In fact, I look forward to it. We seem to have a disagreement that needs to be settled. Kathera's mine and I'll prove it."

The seams of Matthaya's coat began to flex and part as his wings threatened to unfold from his back.

"No!" I reached for his arm.

He glared at me with vibrant, poison-green eyes flickering angrily. "Why not!?" He resisted me. Stitches ripped, the sound making my sensitive ears twitch. "He bit you! He shouldn't be alive right now. Ve'tani saved him so he could torment us! Why shouldn't I put him out of his misery?"

"I'm eager to hear the answer, myself," Derek said, grinning at me.

Our eyes met. The heaviness came over me again, but I fought it back as I stumbled closer to him.

Matthaya stretched an arm out in front of me to block my way. "No," he said. "I won't let you."

"I'm sorry," I said weakly to Derek. "I'm sorry we didn't know you were still alive when we left you there. I'm sorry that woman did this to you. Please, let us be. I've chosen to be with Matthaya. You have to accept that."

"I don't have to accept a damn thing." Derek bared his fangs and bright yellow light burned behind his irises, casting a soft amber glow around his eyes.

I felt Matthaya's temper rising, so I took his hand.

"Leave us alone," I said firmly. "Please."

Derek bit down and his nostrils flared. Then, after a few moments, the anger and hate shaping his face unexpectedly faded away and he composed himself.

"Like I said," he added, glaring at Matthaya, "I'll prove it. But, until then." He tipped his head slightly but didn't break eye contact.

And in a fleeting moment, he vanished into the darkness, the air swiftly cleansed of his presence.

The heaviness left me, and I felt stronger, but my thirst for blood had intensified.

Matthaya's grasp tightened and he squeezed my fingers. Although rage still coiled inside him, he looked over at me and said, "Let's go home. We must satiate your hunger before it consumes you."

6

MATTHAYA

I HAD Kathera sit on the couch while I put on a fire. As a vampire, she needed warmth less than the fire's tranquil ambiance and soothing color. I had to do whatever I could to calm her.

"Wait here," I said, pressing my fingertips against her shoulder. I left the living room to descend down the basement stairs, where I plucked a bottle from the wine rack, and then returned to her. As I crossed the room toward the kitchen, I saw her cradling her face in her hands while hunching over on the seat.

The eruption of psychological pain saturating her

began to infiltrate me, and a storm of agony, frustration, and regret clouded my mind. Derek had never actually died, although I was certain he had bled to death. At the time, I could not hear a heartbeat.

How did he survive? When did Ve'tani come back to retrieve him?

Most importantly—*why?*

Ve'tani was not one for sympathetic plights, but she was always keen on strategy, and his becoming a Taken was likely her retaliating against my taking Kathera.

I twisted the metal spiral of the bottle opener, forcing it down into the cork, and then I turned the handle in the opposite direction and withdrew it. The soft plunking sound of the bottle being opened made Kathera look up; her attention shifted to focus on my actions.

It was not infant blood I poured this time, but it also was not the usual. Since Kathera had wanted to stay in town to work, the inability to travel extensively left the coveted commodity difficult to attain. I made do with what I could acquire. Oftentimes, it was pig blood, and other times, it was something else.

There are those humans with desires for all manner of things of questionable natures. With enough money, you can find anything, without questions. Still, we reduced our intake of young blood, because it was rare and difficult to procure. Kathera had adapted to what I could provide, and we made do with a lack of variety, even though it meant that our hungers would surface more frequently.

"Here." I stretched out an arm and offered her a flute of dark liquid.

"Thank you," she whispered, wrapping her fingers around the stem of the glass; I released it into her grasp. She appeared relieved that it did not smell of swine.

I took a seat beside her on the couch and sipped from my glass.

"I did not know he was still alive when I had urged us to leave," I said, glancing over at her. "If I had—"

"Would you have tried to save him, too?" Kathera looked into my eyes. A glimmer of blood colored her upper lip. "If you'd known?" Her vivid azure irises begged me to respond truthfully.

"I... I could not have saved you both," I replied. "I'm sorry. It took much of my own blood to heal your wounds. I couldn't possibly have done it twice in one night."

"How do you suppose he survived long enough for her to return and..." Kathera took another sip from her glass and swallowed.

"I don't know. Perhaps when Derek stabbed Ve'tani, her blood spilled on him, clotting some of the wounds. Similar to how I saved you, only far less intentional."

"That monster," Kathera growled. "She didn't have to do that to him." She rotated her wrist to reveal the bite mark. It hadn't yet faded but had lightened, leaving traces of purple bruising where his fangs had punctured the skin.

"Vampires do not bite other vampires," I said. "We have no reason to, considering how unsavory vampire blood tastes to our kind. He only did that to prove a point—that you are vulnerable. That you would let him—"

"I'm not vulnerable!" Blue light flashed through her eyes. "I didn't know what to do. All this time, I thought he was dead, and that it was my fault Ve'tani had murdered him. But then I found out he was alive, and emotions and memories clouded my judgment. He took my hand and the next thing I knew, I was trapped in a dream state—a place where there was light and warmth and... *him*. I couldn't control my body or gather the strength to push him away. Not until you arrived and he released me." She fell silent, pressing her lips thin and narrowing her eyes.

"A Sire and Taken may function as one," I said. "But multiple pairs cannot thrive in proximity."

Kathera finished the last of the blood and wiped her thumb across her lip. "He indicated he'd be back," she whispered, a hint of fear rising in her mind as she set the glass down on the end table.

"Ve'tani wants you dead, even now. I'm sure of it. But I won't allow them to take you away from me again." I glanced over at her and brushed my fingertips across her cheek, trying to display a comforting grin; emotions were harder to convey, now that we shared the dampening effects of the disease. "I will fight for you, but I hope it does not come to that. Derek is not as old or evolved as I am. He hasn't tested his limits. If Ve'tani doesn't put him in his place, I will." I stood from the couch and reached over to the table to retrieve her empty glass. "Are you finished?" I asked.

She nodded and then pulled her feet up onto the couch and shifted in place, reclining to lay her head against the armrest.

I turned and made my way back to the kitchen, where I rinsed the two flutes and hung them to dry on a rack above the counter.

By the time I'd returned, Kathera had fallen into a deep sleep on the couch. Her consciousness had faded from my mind as if she'd gone into a hibernation-like state.

The hunger could have done it to her, or the stress.

Or Derek's bite.

I approached slowly and knelt in front of her.

Since being taken, the subtle, pink undertones of life

had left her, leaving her rounded cheeks devoid of delicate color. Shades of blue and purple accented her skin with shadowy, less-than-natural tones. Her hair remained the vivid, dark burgundy red she'd made it, and it framed her innocent round face beautifully still, tumbling over her bare shoulders down to her mid-back.

She looked peaceful, for once. The suicidal nightmares had ceased, but the struggle to continue her art had filled that void, leaving her frustrated and weary. I did what I could to help, but my loyalty and companionship could not break the unrelenting circle of grief and regret feasting upon her soul.

Derek had returned to haunt her, by Ve'tani's command, no doubt. I, too, had been a pet for too long. In the early years, I had listened to and followed my Sire's every command like a hungry stray.

Until I broke free.

Could Derek escape her influence? Did he even desire to?

He'd begun cultivating a deep hatred for me long before he'd been turned, and that festering anger stayed with him, as our last feelings ultimately do.

I glanced over at the fireplace. Flames continued to burn, but the light would do little to comfort her, now that she'd fallen asleep. I came to my feet and crouched down, carefully pushing my hands and arms underneath her so I could lift her up from the couch.

She was lighter than she'd used to be—vampirism had made her body more resilient, but changed the internal structure of her bones and organs, causing much of the water weight to dissolve, as her blood thickened and her veins were less reliant on circulating it.

Kathera didn't stir as I lifted her from the couch and adjusted my grasp on her. I carried her into the bedroom and laid her down on the bed. Not a fragment of her consciousness moved through me.

I walked to the bookshelf beside our bed and slipped out a title. Reading helped pass the time and settle my thoughts, but no words could quiet the turmoil twisting through my brain. I had sworn to keep her safe, but I'd failed her already.

I sat beside her on the bed and clutched the book in my hands. Kathera's innocent face mirrored a slumbering angel painted in oils—a vision of art only a master could conjure. But no master artist could alter the reality lurking behind her placid expression.

7
KATHERA

MATTHAYA'S FINGERS combed through my hair as I slept. His soft touch was comforting, and the safety I felt within his presence allowed me to rest peacefully.

It was quiet in my mind.

The emptiness gave me room to create. It was the calm before the storm, when fantastic visions and wild creatures would appear, frolicking across the dream-scape of my consciousness.

But from that sanctified place of serenity and inspiration, vile things emerged.

ꝏ   ᘓ

A familiar scent teased my nostrils and I eased my eyes open. Matthaya was gone and the space beside me on the bed was empty.

"You won't find him here," a voice spoke from the other side of the room.

I rolled over. A flicker of amber light emanated from Derek's eyes as he stood in the shadows at the threshold of the room.

"How did you...?" My limbs were numb and weak and I strained to sit up.

Derek crossed the room and sat beside me on the bed. He reached over to drag his hand up my bare arm. The touch felt unusually warm against my skin, unlike Matthaya's.

Unlike... *any* vampire.

I tried again to move, but an invisible force restricted me, barely allowing me to come up onto my elbows.

"What's the hurry?" Derek asked, smirking. His fangs weren't visible at all.

"Y-you shouldn't be here," I said, trembling as his fingers inched toward my neck.

"You want me here, though, don't you?" he asked in a softer tone, leaning over me.

I...

I couldn't reply.

My arms shook and gave out, making me slip onto my back. Derek climbed onto the bed and came down onto all fours, positioning himself over me and pinning me in place with his weight as he straddled my legs. He leaned down, his breath warm against my neck, and I flinched, my back arching as I tried to wriggle out from under him.

He pushed the hem of my shirt up and the flaps of his open button-up shirt tickled my bare midriff.

I bit down in resistance, barely able to utter a firm "no."

But he didn't hesitate at all, and instead lathed his tongue across my abdomen, while inching his fingers up my side.

I reached up to grasp onto his shoulders, but weakness overcame me and I couldn't find the strength to dig my nails into his skin.

He kissed the side of my ribcage, and I sucked in a sharp breath.

Matthaya... Matthaya... Please. Help me.

I had to get away from Derek.

Wake up! Wake up!

I must have been asleep.

It was just a nightmare. It wasn't real.

His warm-blooded touch seemed real, as did the distinct aroma of his skin.

He let up, slightly, and I felt his eyes on me. Subtle movement drew me to meet his gaze and I gasped in horror as Derek's features and clothing began to transform.

An eerie gray color swept over his skin. A crisp, black suit jacket unfolded down his back and sides, as his shirt turned white and long sleeves stretched down to his wrists. Then his hair grew longer, dark waves falling to the base of his neck.

"Is this really how you want it to go?" he asked. His face and clothing mirrored Matthaya's.

"No!" I still couldn't move. Sickness pooled in my stomach and a new kind of fear shook me. Even the smell of his skin had changed to mimic the woodsy, damp petrichor I'd grown to recognize from my husband.

But his eyes told the truth. They weren't the beautiful green of the man I had married. They were the deepest, most sinister brown.

Then he smiled—a big, toothy grin with bright, lengthy incisors gleaming, longer and more pronounced than any I'd seen.

"Derek, stop!" I hissed, pushing against him with all my might, though he didn't budge. "You're not Matthaya!"

"This was your idea," he said with a sarcastic smile,

running his tongue across his fangs. "I'm up for a little role play." He raised an eyebrow. "I'll be Matthaya and you can be..." His fingernail traced a line across my throat. "Well, *you*." He shrugged and cocked his head to the side. "Come on. You can't tell me you haven't wanted *this*—that you can turn down the opportunity to do what you couldn't before. I can offer you that. In the real world, we can't feel pain... or pleasure. We can't enjoy passion or warmth... or sex. Lucky for you, you're not in that world anymore. You're in mine. Here, you can have whatever, and do whoever, you want. Even him, if that's what you really want from me."

"I don't want anything from you!" I squirmed and grunted beneath his weight.

He was frightening! Damn him, he was frightening.

"You've changed, Derek!" I tried, one more time, to force him off me but couldn't. Some unseen force had me paralyzed. "Stop this, please." My feebleness enraged me.

He wrapped his fingers around my wrists and pressed them back and deep into the bed, chuckling as fierce golden sparkle ignited his eyes.

"You *don't* want me?" he said gruffly, but with the distinct velvet cadence of Matthaya's voice. "You don't want to be with your husband?"

He *wasn't* Matthaya.

But Derek looked, and even smelled, like him now. The man holding me down on that bed *was*, to all my other senses, Matthaya.

"Let me go." I groaned, turning my face to the side and squeezing my eyes closed to avoid his gaze. "I don't want you."

"What's that?" He bent closer until his weight pressed against my chest. "Now why would you say a thing like that? You... ungrateful..." His lips hovered over my ear and his breath turned cold. "I am yours," he whispered, nibbling my ear. "And you are mine."

I made the mistake of opening my eyes. Vivid, neon green mixed with fluorescent yellow electrified his irises as his jaws separated.

"No!" I screamed, but the word was cut short by teeth sinking into my throat. He bit down—hard—and it cut off the air from my lungs. Hot blood spilled over my skin and the pressure of his weight suffocated me.

I'd been bitten once, but it wasn't the same. I don't remember it well, but my flesh had remained attached to my body.

Not this time.

Pain shredded through me as he latched onto my neck like a lion. He let up momentarily and I trembled, shaking from the icy sensation enveloping me, making my fingertips tingle and lose feeling. He came down for a second bite. His teeth dug deeper and his bite clamped down harder, until I thought I would lose consciousness.

I *hoped* I would.

Blood spewed from the wound, splashing crimson on his white shirt.

Then I was forced to taste it as it dripped into my mouth. Iron. Bitterness. Death.

I gasped, gagging on my own blood.

Pain shot through my veins like acid, burning between freezing chills.

I was dying.

I strained to take a breath, but no air would come in.

He sat back on his heels and dragged his sleeve across his face, slicking blood from his chin.

I brought a hand up to my neck to put pressure on the massive wound. The ribs of my esophagus prickled my fingers.

The bleeding wouldn't stop.

He looked down at me, his eyes brighter than ever from the fever of his bloody feast. He trailed his fingers down my neck, tracing a red streak across my collarbone and down toward my cross necklace.

He smiled, twisting the chain around his blood-covered hand. "You should pray, Kathera."

"St-op." I coughed up blood.

He dropped the pendant back onto my chest and let out a heavy sigh.

"You just don't get it, do you?" A grimace curled in his lips. "Matthaya stole you from me." He narrowed his eyes. "Now I'm taking you back."

He didn't... steal me...

Derek's words hurt like hell.

But so did the gaping fatal gash he had torn in my throat.

8

MATTHAYA

KATHERA WRITHED in her sleep, muttering incoherently as if possessed. I couldn't feel what she was dreaming about and was suddenly unable to reach into her mind to see for myself.

"Kathera." I tried waking her with a few firm nudges, but she wouldn't come out of the fit.

I leaned over her and grasped her arms.

"Kathera! Wake up."

Her seizures made her difficult to hold on to; I had to brace myself to keep a firm grip on her.

I closed my eyes and tried to connect with her mind

again, pressing through the dense barrier of rampant, ricocheting thoughts. Her consciousness was clouded with noise and I couldn't break through all the commotion.

Then she went still and silent and a vivid burst of color flooded my brain as she returned to me.

Her eyes opened and wild blue light permeated her irises. She screamed, pulled free, and then slammed her hands into me, thrusting me off the bed and onto the floor. The forceful thud rattled me, and I took a moment to come to my feet.

"Are you all right?" I asked, nearing the bedside.

She scrambled back against the headboard while cupping both hands around her throat. Bright, widened eyes gazed out at nothing, and she was petrified and speechless.

I slowly took a step closer.

"I-I..." She lowered her hands from her throat and hastily looked them over. "I'm not bleeding anymore. Am I?" she asked, touching her neck again and then checking her fingers a second time.

"No. You aren't bleeding at all," I said quietly.

"But... I saw it. He..." She bit down and grimaced, folding over as she grasped her other wrist tightly and pulled it close to her chest. It was the one Derek had bitten.

"What has he done to you?" I asked, sensing a myriad of thoughts involving him coiling through her. I continued to try to pry into her memories and uncover the traumatizing dream, but I couldn't get through.

She looked up at me, her eyes no longer aglow, and sat with her mouth agape.

"I don't know. I thought I was dreaming," she said, her voice breaking.

"That was no ordinary dream," I corrected. "I could not reach you in that state. Please tell me what happened. What did you see?" I took another step closer and she cringed, almost as if she were frightened of *me*.

"You..." She cupped her hands around her neck again and pushed her heels into the mattress as she scooted back.

A fleeting vision of her throat being torn out, by a dark figure, flashed into my mind. I bit down and growled, baring my fangs unintentionally toward her; she shrieked.

Her anxiety and fear buzzed through my body, forcing my anger to subside. How could she be afraid of me!?

"It's okay now," I said in a hushed tone, shaking off the rage that had ignited my eyes. "Did he do that to you in your vision?"

"No." She lifted her gaze toward me, paused briefly

to process her thoughts, and then uttered, "You did."

Me?!

"The man in your visions could not have been—"

"No," she corrected. "No. It wasn't *you*. It was..." She twisted her wrist inward and shuddered. "Derek. He turned into you so that he could..."

Pain sizzled through her nerves, sending residual waves through my own body. The impulses made my fingers twitch, the sensation resembling an intolerable itch deep beneath my skin.

Kathera grunted and doubled over, cradling her wrist. "It hurts," she bellowed through clenched teeth.

But vampires do not feel pain.

Irritation and discomfort, perhaps, but we cannot process *actual* pain. Not as humans know it.

The unsettling twinge creeping beneath my skin, on behalf of our connection, was *indeed* reminiscent of pain.

"Let me see the mark." I put an open hand toward her. She lifted her arm and cautiously offered it toward me.

I examined the bite. Hairline forks of deep purple and maroon color spread out from the central punctures; I'd never seen anything like it.

"It's so painful," she said hoarsely. "Can you make it stop?"

Anger billowed inside me. I looked over the mark a

second time. My first theory was that Ve'tani had created, once again, a new Sire. If so, he shouldn't have been able to gain control over Kathera, as my own DNA had already compromised her system and we were not susceptible to being "re-sired," as far as I knew. But then, I'd never allowed myself to be bitten by another Sire. Nor was such a thing customary.

A quick sniff of her skin proved me wrong instantly. She still smelled the same, and our minds were still fully linked, despite the brief lapse in our connection earlier.

The veins spreading from the wound were forking in several directions, carrying the color through her body like a virus.

No.

Like poison.

"I think Derek poisoned you," I said.

"No." Kathera jerked her arm away. "That's not possible, is it? Why would he?"

"Every human's DNA is impacted differently by the disease. I do not know the extent of the effects vampirism can have on any one individual. You've seen what it did to me."

"It was a dream—a nightmare," she muttered in denial.

"As are my wings to some."

"No." She shook her head. "I've had them before.

Bad things often happen in my dreams. You know that."

"But this is different," I replied. "I couldn't reach you as you slept. It was as though you were no longer in sync with me and I had lost the ability to connect with your consciousness. His venom severed our ties long enough for him to control your dream; I won't let him get away with this."

I narrowed my eyes and squeezed a fist. My wings wriggled with agitation and anticipation of a fight. I swerved away from her and took a step toward the door.

"I'll..."

"No!" Kathera grabbed onto my sleeve, halting me.

I turned back to see her kneeling at the foot of the bed, her arm outstretched and her fingers clutching my jacket. "Please, don't go after him. I sense your anger, and I know it's there with good reason, but... please don't go."

I refused to make promises I might break, so I remained silent and still.

"Please," she continued. "The pain is letting up. He made his point. Let's just forget about him for now."

"How can I forget?" I asked. My brows furrowed and the desire for revenge made me restless. "Why should I ignore what he did to you—what he did to my *wife*!?"

She slid off the bed and took both my hands. Her rich blue eyes pleaded for sympathy. "Because he's suffering, too," she said.

The anger in me began to diminish almost instantly, upon hearing those words from her lips. Kathera was newly changed, but enough of her humanity remained that she could still see him for what he was—a pawn in Ve'tani's petty war against us.

"Ve'tani took him, and he's confused and angry, just like I was, at first. Just like *you* were, at first." Her fingers slid between mine. "Maybe, even frightened."

She spoke with great wisdom, but...

"You were not under Ve'tani's counsel," I countered. "She is a monster, and she will shape him into one. Wouldn't it be more merciful to save him from a torturous eternity with her?"

"No!" Radiant blue light flashed through Kathera's eyes. "*We* allowed him to die once. I won't let him die again."

I pressed my lips thin and hesitated. "As long as he remains with *her*, he's as good as dead."

Her brow wrinkled, and then a glimmer of hope curled her lips. "But, what if she chooses another? What if she decides to take someone else? Will he be free?"

It was not so simple.

"No," I answered. "He would become an *Abandoned One*—one forsaken by a Sire to allow for a new companion. Abandoned Ones' connections with their Sires are shattered once a new Taken is chosen, and the influx of noise in the disconnected mind leaves them disoriented and vulnerable. They cannot be reclaimed by another, nor can they survive on their own."

"So if Ve'tani chooses someone else, Derek will suffer again?"

I nodded.

"Oh..." Her grasp loosened. "Well, is there anything we can do to help him?"

"We must let nature run its course—however unpredictable or cruel. It is the only thing we can do. I know this is not what you may want to hear, but for your own good, you must stay away from him."

She opened her mouth to reply, but I sternly interrupted with, "You must."

Pain and regret swirled through her mind, and disappointment weighed heavily on her heart.

"I understand," she uttered.

9
MATTHAYA

WE'D REACHED a stalemate; there was no agreeable way for us to deal with Derek's behavior.

The unspoken fear that her dreams could be seized again by him kept me on edge. The physical mark on her wrist was fading, but the emotional damage remained.

Her ruminating made me apprehensive, too, as her feelings often bled into my own, making me lose track of my thoughts. This forced me to look for a way to keep her occupied and focused on something other than *him*.

I sat on an antique velvet chair in the foyer and spun my signet ring around my finger. Kathera had suggested we research its origin, but it never truly interested me, and so I never made an effort.

The gold shimmered beneath the dim light of the table lamp beside me, the emerald glistening with vivid shades of greenish-blue. The hand-forged gold dragons embellishing the band were family crests of some kind. Inside the band, I found no hallmark.

I looked up; from where I sat, I could see into the kitchen. On the edge of the countertop was Kathera's laptop, primarily used for researching designs and emailing clients. I pushed up out of my chair and made my way over to it.

The shop kept us busy, and even without taking many appointments, she filled her week with the toils of designing and inking tattoos, while I took care of the paperwork and general bills. It wasn't the type of work that consumed my entire day, but I often pretended it did, in an effort to appear as supportive of her career as possible. I was at her beck and call, but I could easily do more to free up her precious time.

"Kathera?" I called to her. She was in the bedroom, sketching. Each pen stroke weaved through my mind as if it were my own, and I envisioned the new design coming to life at her hand. At least she was trying again, though some level of discord and disappointment kept her from feeling satisfaction from any recent work.

She stopped drawing and came to find me.

"Yes?" She walked into the kitchen and tipped her head when she saw me standing beside her computer. "Are you looking for something?"

I was not particularly fond of electronics, but they were a necessity to get anything done efficiently in the modern era. Information was available at the click of a button—knowledge that often took months, if not years, to ascertain in the days before the internet.

"I would like your help." I slid the heavy signet ring off my finger and offered it to her. "I would like to begin researching this, but I don't know where to start."

"Of course, but..." She cocked an eyebrow. "Why the sudden interest? I'd mentioned it before, but you—"

"I've been thinking about *us*, and I believe it is only right for you to know more about the man you married."

"Oh." She glanced at the ring and a small smile curled her lips. The expression, though subtle, cut through some of the darkness in her heart. "I would love to help you research it."

"Thank you." I set the ring down beside the touch-pad of her laptop. "I did not find any etchings inside the band, if that helps."

"A little, I think. I was about to suggest you search for an artist's mark." She pulled up one of the nearby barstools so she could sit at the raised counter, and then gestured for me to do the same and sit beside her.

"Where was Kathryn born?" she asked.

"Ulster province, though I can't recall the exact county. Her father's land kissed the ocean shore."

"And how old were you when they took you in?"

"Six, I believe. I suppose I was born in 1600."

She opened a web browser and navigated to a search engine, where she typed in the province and my birth year.

"This was during the Nine Years' War," she said, pointing to a color-coded map of English and Irish territories and settlements. "It looks like much of it was under British occupation, at the time, but there were a few Irish clans holding residences outside this occupied area." She pointed at a section of sparse purple, representing rogue Irish settlements. "Do any of these county or city names sound familiar to you?"

I grazed over the extensive, rather colorful list, but nothing jogged my memory. "No, but then I cannot remember much of my childhood before meeting Kathryn."

"Then I'll try something different," she replied, not losing morale over my lack of details. I waited as she swiftly typed in some other terms and navigated at lightning speed to a series of other pages—encyclopedias of Irish clan coat-of-arms. "Maybe there's something here that will help guide us." She pointed to the switch beside the kitchen faucet. "Turn on the main light, please."

I stood and then crossed the narrow hall to flip the switch, illuminating the room with fair yellow light. Our hunting instincts allowed us to see movement and prey well in low light, but the fine details of the ring escaped us.

She lifted the ring toward the light and rotated it slowly. "The dragon has two wings, three horns, and a tail with an arrow-head point at the tip." She squinted and held the ring a little closer to the lamp. "There's a distinct bend in the tail. Do you see that? It looks like a snail shell or a coil of some kind, only it has square angles." The ring moved into my line of sight and she held it there a moment. "That design in the tail, isn't that weird?"

"I believe that is a variation of a Celtic rune," I said, taking the ring into my own fingers. "I don't recognize it." I skimmed over the shape, following the lines back to the large emerald. "The prongs," I said, "they, too, have etchings on them—the same rune."

Kathera scrolled down several dozen images of heraldic crests featuring Celtic dragons, shaking her head because none of them appeared to resemble the one on my ring.

"I'm not sure where else we could look," she said. "There are so many variations, and not having a firm starting point will make it difficult to narrow these down." She shifted on her stool and reached a hand up to grasp her cross pendant, tangling the chain gently around her fingers, as she sometimes did when she was thinking intently. "The library may have something more useful. Maybe a book related to the specific time period and region. Or the museum downtown. They have a small archive collection from Ireland. I remember seeing it when I was there on a field trip back in middle school. I don't know if it's still there, but—" Her face came up and she dropped her pendant. "Wait." She stood from the seat. "I have an idea. Come with me."

I followed her into the living room where she brought me over to Kathryn's painting and gestured toward it. "Would you mind taking it down from the mantel so I can look at it?"

I was hesitant at first, but then carefully reached up and grasped the old oil painting by the sides and lifted it from the shelf. "Where would you like me to put it?"

"Right here is fine," she said, kneeling down on the rug in front of the fireplace.

I knelt, too, and placed the painting carefully before us.

Kathera sighed and leaned over the painting, her fingers inching toward the cross pendant hanging from Kathryn's neck—the exact one Kathera now wore. "I...

never really looked at her this closely before," she whispered, raising her hand to clasp her necklace again. "This painting and this necklace both survived over 400 years because of you." She smiled at me. "Thank you for keeping them safe."

"I did everything I could to protect them." I reached to touch her hand. "And I will do whatever it takes to protect you, too."

Kathera released the cross. "I know." She leaned over Kathryn's painting and her gaze traced the perimeter of the canvas.

"What is it you're looking for?" I asked.

"A signature or something to indicate who the artist was." Her finger hovered over the painting as she searched. "Do you remember anything about the painter?"

I thought hard and only one tiny detail came to mind. "He had a strange accent. I do remember thinking that, at the time."

"Strange? As in?"

"I was preoccupied with not being caught watching him work while I did my chores, so I don't remember anything else."

"Here!" She pointed to a scribble of dark paint on the corner of Kathryn's sleeve.

"Armand?" I read out loud.

"Is that what it says?" She cocked her head and peered

more closely at the sloppy signature. "I can't read that."

"The A is there." I pointed to the top of the shape and then the crossbar. "And the D. It's difficult to read, but the M is legible if you ignore the extraneous R between the first two letters. I've heard that name before. It could be French."

"Or German," Kathera added. "My father was friends with a man from Germany with the same name."

"French or German, what does this artist have to do with me?"

"Back then, skilled painters often traveled to do work for hire. Maybe this one traveled around Ireland doing paintings for different families. Maybe he worked for someone from the same village where you were born. It's a little bit of a stretch, I know, but I don't know where else to begin. We have to use the information we have on hand. This painting—the artist—it's a time stamp. It will give me a starting point."

The deep blue color of her eyes pulled me in, and I could see now how very passionate she was about discovering where I'd come from, even though I did not share that enthusiasm.

"This is very important to you, isn't it?" I asked, gazing fondly at the sudden spark of interest lighting her smile.

"It is. Occupying my time with this research will

help keep my mind off Derek. Maybe switching my focus to something completely different will give me time to recharge and find my creative fire again."

I briefly thought to tell her that she might never find that creative fire again—that the disease was not kind to our passions, and that vampirism could drain her soul over time, siphoning out most, if not all, of her creative energy.

I couldn't.

Those words were harsh, and the reality too dark for her now.

And even hypocritical.

If I could experience love toward Kathera, then she might retain some of the artistic ambience our disease threatens to take away. I did not know all there was to know about our kind, so I would leave it to her to prove me wrong in my assumptions.

"Shall I go with you? To the library? Or the museum?" I asked.

For a moment, I thought she might say no, but she must have sensed my apprehension about her wandering around town alone with Derek on the loose.

"You can come, but they close early each day, so I am not sure it will work out that way."

Kathera could expose herself to sunlight as if she had never been turned, and that limited my ability to accompany her, at times. It had made me unsettled at first—but I learned to let it go and accept the gift for what it was. *Hers.*

"We will find a way to make it work for us both," I replied confidently. I lifted Kathryn's painting and placed it carefully atop the mantel, adjusting it to rest against the wall.

I turned to Kathera, who was staring at the portrait with a sorrowful expression.

"What's wrong?" I asked.

She veered toward me as if I'd surprised her somehow.

"What were you thinking?" I could have simply pried into her mind to find out, but I chose to not. She deserved privacy, and I wanted to give her space and freedom from our binding—sometimes invasive—connection.

She looked at the painting and smiled bittersweetly. "She was beautiful," she answered. "Do you see much of her in me?"

"I don't need to see her in you in order to love you." I brushed my fingers across her brow, sweeping her bangs to the side. "You, Kathera, were shaped by this era. Regardless of the ties you may have with her, you are not Kathryn, and you need not feel pressured to be like her."

Kathera looked off to the side and a twinge of sadness spiraled through her mind.

"You're beautiful," I continued, lifting her face back toward me. "When I look at you, I see my wife—the woman I love."

She smiled, and I sensed some of her doubts lifting.

10

MATTHAYA

KATHERA SAT on the couch in the living room with her laptop balanced atop her knees. Her studies had taken her long into the night, until brilliant beams of sunlight framed the window, overflowing from the blackout curtains.

"How are you feeling?" I asked.

She lifted her gaze from her monitor. "I'm having a hard time focusing," she said. The dark shadows around her eyes were a shade deeper than usual, and noticeably redder. I did not sense a thirst for blood rising in her, but it was possible she needed it anyway.

"Do you hunger?" I asked.

"No." Her eyes met the glowing screen again and the cool white light illuminated her face.

"Do you think you need rest?" I approached her side and bent toward her. "Kathera?"

Her exhausted gaze met mine again. "I wanted to keep searching... but..."

We did not need much sleep, but I feared Derek's bite was making her lethargic.

I carefully pressed my fingers to the back of her laptop screen and pushed it closed.

"But..." she began, as I lifted the computer away from her.

"History isn't going anywhere. You can continue your research after you get some energy back. It is more important that you rest and recover. Your mind needs it, too."

"I'll be fine," she replied, narrowing her eyes skeptically at me. "Why are you so worried? It's not like I'm in danger of sleep deprivation anymore."

I didn't want to tell her, but the color of her eyes appeared gray-blue now, and the intensity of her under eye shadows planted new fears in me. Something was off, even if she wouldn't admit it.

But she sensed my fears even before I could respond, and a look of concern twisted her lips. "I'll sleep then," she uttered. "Where will you be?"

"Here, of course. I'll stay right here," I said, gesturing to the chair beside her as I set her computer on the nearby coffee table.

She resituated herself on the couch on her side, stretched out, and tucked a small pillow under her neck.

I contemplated retrieving a blanket for her comfort. While many senses had been dampened by the disease, simple mortal pleasures sometimes soothed what little humanity remained inside us.

I looked over at her. "Would you like a..." She'd closed her eyes. I pressed my hand onto hers, but she didn't respond; her consciousness had gone silent.

It was the fastest I'd ever seen her fall asleep, and that made me suspicious.

I sat beside her and retrieved her computer from the table. As I opened the lid, I noticed several icons on her desktop with various titles, as well as folders for different things, such as crests, cities, and surnames. There was a document titled "links" there, too. I clicked it. There were at least a hundred URLs on the list, each labeled with a small description typed by her.

I'd barely had the time to pay bills and take care of Kieran's wages, and somehow, she had been able to do extensive research.

Kathera was much better at utilizing the internet

than I was.

Keeping up with technology never was my strongest asset. Not because I was incapable, but because I chose not to care. Technology comes and goes in flashes while Mother Nature carries on at a steady pace.

My wings twitched under my shirt, longing to be stretched. It had been a long time since I'd allowed them that freedom. Kathera had asked to see them a few times since I'd rescued her, but I kept them tucked away. They are a constant reminder of what I am—a beast, a creature of the night designed only to take life, not to give it.

I pushed the urge aside, as I had many times before, and filtered through some of the notations in her documents. Another folder contained a series of images featuring various etchings of dragons on jewelry made in the 17th century. None of them looked anything like the one on my ring. A wyvern—a long, snake-like dragon with no front legs. A European dragon with four legs and two wings, but no horns. None of them featured strange twists in the tail or an extra horn.

There was also a folder of some runes and their interpretations. I clicked on it and began scrolling through the images.

I had only viewed a few pictures when a shudder of fear jolted through my mind.

I veered toward Kathera; her hands were tensed and

her body convulsing.

"Kathera!" I set the laptop aside and shot up from my seat. I wrapped my hands around her shoulders and tried to steady her, but she continued to shake, the seizure consuming her. I closed my eyes and willed myself into her mind, forcing my consciousness into hers so that I could witness what was going on.

At first, it was dark and I was unable to pass through the heavy blackness of her thoughts. I tried again, releasing all inhibitions, freeing the Sire in me to take hold of her mind, like I was meant to.

The shadow began to dissipate and my consciousness breached the barrier. I found her—a physical representation of herself—in an imaginary setting deep inside her thoughts.

"Matthaya!?" She stood at the back of a long, beige corridor, dimly lit by sputtering fluorescent lamps dangling from the ceiling. She clasped onto her shoulders and shivered. "It's so cold here," she said. "Where are we?"

I took a step toward her and the hall suddenly lengthened, forcing us another several yards apart.

A deep growl reverberated in my throat and, before I considered other options, I bolted after her.

The room stretched again, dizzying and disorienting me. I slid to a halt, braced myself, and lunged once more.

And again, like an accordion, the hallway stretched, pulling her out of reach.

"Matthaya!" she cried out, her voice shrinking into the distance.

I removed my jacket and roared angrily, willing my feral wings to come free. They snapped open with a powerful flap, catching on the sides of the narrow hall, the clawed tips tearing gashes through tattered drywall.

Kathera took a step toward me, and a dark shadow manifested between us, blocking her path. The wispy cloud of inky black shifted and warped until it formed a human shape and became opaque.

Derek.

How had he infiltrated Kathera's mind with me there?

"What are you doing here?" I snarled, approaching him. The room didn't move this time. Over his shoulder, I saw Kathera rushing toward us. "Get out of her head!" My wings curled inward and trembled anxiously. Another few inches and I could have taken his head clean-off with them.

"Why don't *you*?" He took a step closer to me. "It's my turn."

My wings became incredibly stiff and the joints tightened as I attempted to move them. I tried to take a step, but I was pushed back by an unseen force.

Derek grinned.

How had he gained control over this place in Kathera's mind, and how had I lost my power over her? Even as her Sire, I was unable to stop Derek's actions.

Behind him, Kathera was still far in the distance of the darkened hallway, the light illuminating her like an eerie spotlight.

"Why are you doing this to her?" I asked, trying once again to move, but my wings locked up and my legs were frozen in place.

Derek took another step closer, well in range of my attack—had I been able to move.

"I'm just taking back what's mine," he hissed. "You should go. You have no power here."

"I'll kill you!" I growled, baring my fangs. Colored light fringed his silhouette as my hunting instincts kicked in.

"Did you not hear what I just said?" Derek came closer and looked me right in the eye. His dark brows furrowed spitefully as gold light shimmered in his irises. "You can't hurt—"

One of my wings broke free.

It sliced through the air, cutting a deep gash across Derek's cheek, which sent him reeling to the side, stumbling into the wall and struggling to catch his balance.

Before a sense of triumph could come over me, Kathera screamed and tumbled to her knees, holding her face in her hands as blood leaked through her fingers.

The echo of her painful cry thrust me from her mind, snapping me back into reality.

We were in the living room again—our living room, just the two of us.

I was arched over her sleeping body as she lay on the couch, a line of dark burgundy blood oozing down her cheek from a fresh wound.

But my wings were still tucked away in my back, hidden beneath my jacket.

How?

"Stay out of this." Derek's voice echoed in my mind. "Or she'll be the one to pay."

I bit down and growled, causing Kathera to stir in her sleep. She wriggled and writhed on the couch, but seemed to be straining to wake up.

"Kathera?" I pressed my hands onto her cheeks and gently tilted her face toward me.

Her mind was dark and remained far from my grasp. Derek had blocked me out now and taken ahold of her, forcing her into some sort of mental paralysis.

Blood drizzled toward her jawline and I slicked it away with my thumb.

I bent down until my face was close to hers and quickly ran my tongue across the wound, covering it with a thin layer of saliva that made it instantly sizzle and heal. It would have healed on its own—eventually—but I didn't want to take a chance of her waking to it before then. I had no way of knowing how little or how much of the "dream" she would remember.

Intense bitterness made me grimace, and the taste of her vampire blood turned my stomach. But it was a small price to pay, as the horror of whatever Derek was doing in her mind continued to play out without me, and there was nothing I could do but stand there as she battled a monster in her head.

Why was he doing this to her, and how?

Only a Sire and Taken have a psychological bridge, and yet he'd been able to hijack ours and divert my attack on him there onto her physical body.

I would not stand there and let him manipulate her any longer.

I wouldn't let Ve'tani's newest creation tear my wife apart.

11

MATTHAYA

SINCE I'D severed ties with my Sire, I could not pick up even a semblance of Ve'tani's scent or a blip of imagery from my prior mental connection with her.

Not a single lead in sight or in mind, and that posed a problem in my search to find her.

I knew Ve'tani well enough, though. Her fetishes for compliments and good fights compelled her to linger in red-light districts. There, she could find easy prey and feed her vanity. I'd been living in the city long enough to know where to find such a place.

Past the cemetery. Past Restless Ink. Past a row of

downtrodden homes in desperate need of repair. To a stretch of sidewalk lit with colorful neon signs and pavement thundering with the vibration of bass music pouring out of nearby clubs.

I passed a rotating glass door with a large, muscular man in a spike-studded leather vest standing guard. He eyed me up, all too eager to send away anyone who didn't fit the dress code or couldn't pay the cover.

It was different now than it once was. In the early years of my vampirism, Ve'tani and I preyed on poor inebriated bastards who had no friends to guide them home at dawn. Those lost causes with no family, and no job to return to in the morning. Desperate, forlorn souls at wit's end.

Ve'tani would speak of "excess" population and "culling the herd," and she was proud.

I wasn't proud of any of it.

They were easy victims, but the alcohol saturating their blood made them unappealing. We did not always have an opportunity to be picky, and she made many excuses for why we should feed upon the downtrodden over the rich and, frankly, better tasting humans.

She also enjoyed posh company and lush compliments, something she'd get more often from the upperclass partygoers, so she tended to leave them alone. Feeding her ego came first.

A couple popped out through the door of one of the bars and I tipped my face to the side to avoid eye contact with them as they staggered past me, laughing.

What was I thinking, walking these questionable parts of town as if I'd had a chance at finding her? In a city of nearly one million, how did I expect to find only one?

I turned a corner and walked down another block. With each passing minute, I grew more antsy and concerned about Kathera. She'd be safe in our home, but knowing Derek was out there somewhere, traumatizing her from a distance, made me furious.

I had to find them. Or I had to convince them to find me.

"Ve'tani!" I shouted up at the sky, and the sound quickly died in the atmosphere. If she were anywhere nearby—even a few miles away—she'd hear me. I sniffed the air, hoping to get a trace of something that might point me in the right direction.

Nothing.

I crossed the road and headed down a lengthy backstreet snaking behind a grocery store. The dark stretch of loading docks littered with broken grocery carts appeared devoid of people.

Trying to find Ve'tani in the enormous city, without so much as a single clue, was futile. With no idea where else to search, and my concern for Kathera growing stronger, I finally took a turn down another block and headed home.

The walk back was quiet and uneventful, but the moment I turned the corner by Restless Ink, my senses piqued, and I caught a glimpse of a shadowy figure moving in the distance. It paused as soon as it saw me.

I approached the shop cautiously and waited for them to make a move, remaining calm in case they were human.

"You look as though you are searching for someone," a familiar raspy voice spoke. Ve'tani moved out from beneath the awning and onto the dimly lit sidewalk. Her bangles jingled with each step.

"I... *was*." I composed myself and tried to hide my uneasiness. "What do you want?"

"I thought you were looking for me," she said, lowering the hood of her cloak. Curls of straw-colored blonde hair glistened beneath the streetlamp. "I heard you beckon my name from the depths of the city. What an appalling part of town, may I add. No class, whatsoever anymore."

"Why didn't you come?" I asked.

She cocked an eyebrow at me. "I am not your pet. I did not feel like wasting my energy. I knew you would be back here. Although..." Her index finger rose to tap her lower lip. "You seem quite ungrateful I even bothered to wait for you. Perhaps I should go." She turned.

"No!" I nearly lunged for her velvet cloak but stopped myself before I could make the desperate move. "Please... wait."

"Ah." She turned and grinned villainously. "Did I just hear you say 'please'?" She rolled her eyes. "What dire predicament would force you to use such niceties with me?"

"Derek," I replied gruffly. "He's out of control. You must stop him."

"Stop him?" She cackled. "What makes you think *I* can control him at all? I could not even control *you*. Derek will do as he pleases, and only after he satiates his feral desires will he return to willfully accept his place beside me. You should know that much, Matthaya."

"I'll kill him," I seethed. "If you don't get him under control, I'll kill him."

"Do as you wish," she replied with a shrug. "He means nothing to me. He was an opportunity, and it seems my decision to save him has made your life hell. It is what you deserve for abandoning me for that... girl."

"I didn't know I was a Sire until you tried to murder Kathera, forcing me to do whatever I could to save her. You brought this upon yourself. Now tell me where to find Derek."

"I don't know." She shrugged again and laughed.

"Liar!"

Her bright yellow-orange eyes glistened angrily at me. "Oh, if I knew, I wouldn't be wasting my time here!"

"How is he doing it?" I asked.

"Doing what?" She narrowed her eyes as if she'd had no idea what I was talking about.

"How is he getting into Kathera's mind?"

"Into her—" She drew her head back with surprise. "That is a very interesting accusation." She toyed with a lock of her curly hair. "But it would explain why I cannot seem to distance myself from you two, try as I might. The essence of Kathera's consciousness lingers in the back of my mind, and with it, a sliver of your own."

"He bit her," I added spitefully.

Her eyes expressed shock for a split second before she pretended to not be affected.

"Bit her, you say?" she repeated, intrigued. "Well, that is different."

"Now he's manipulating her—haunting her in her sleep."

"Then why not pop into her consciousness and throw him out?"

"I can't. I tried."

Ve'tani gazed at me intently.

"He's blocking me from reaching her. I tried to stop him, but all it did was get Kathera hurt. Tell me where he is and I'll—"

"I can not." She crossed her arms. "Even if I did know where he was at this very moment, which I do not, I would have no reason to tell you."

I darted toward her, but she stood her ground, unyielding.

"I could kill you, too," I said through clenched teeth, with eyes glinting green. "I could kill you both." The thought of it was almost... satisfying.

"How do you think your wife would feel about that?" She sneered at me. "Killing the man who took care of her when *you* abandoned her. How would she feel if you murdered the man she *might* have married?"

I hissed. "She had no intention of marrying him!"

"Is that the truth?" Ve'tani raised an eyebrow and grinned. "Or is that what she told you?"

"She... told... me..."

"You can never be too careful. We women do not always say what we mean. I would think twice before going after him. Unless you want to lose her *again*."

"Damn it!" I huffed angrily. "Why are you so horrible?"

"I beg to differ," she snarled. "Do you think I enjoy intermittent visions of Derek's newfound fetish twisting through my brain? I. Do. Not. And the sooner he stops, the sooner I can move on and leave this despicable place for good."

"Why don't you leave him now? Why not abandon him and look for another? Since you obviously despise him so much already."

"*Despise* is a strong word for it," she replied, pressing the fingertips of both hands together. "He is a nuisance, yes, but he is not as gifted as you. I may be fond of the idea of having finally sired a vampire with a little less thirst for power. He will be controllable in time. I am certain of that. He is not what you were, but that may not be all bad.

"Kathera will survive whatever Derek chooses to do to her and, in time, he will grow bored of the game. If I were you, Matthaya, I would let it run its course."

"You want me to let him do this to her? She's been through enough hell already and I would never—"

"What is a bit more, then?" she asked with a cruel smile.

"If you don't get him under control, I will." I clenched my fists. "And don't think I'm above killing *you* to stop him."

Ve'tani let out a brief, un-ladylike snort of laughter. "I do not think you are above *anything*." She clicked her tongue. "I also do not believe you." She turned, tossed her hood back up over her head, and then sprinted off into the darkness.

She had proved her point. I did not pursue her, though I considered it.

The thought of killing her was tempting, but it wasn't the solution. She was strong, and she wouldn't go down without a long, bloody fight. I couldn't risk my own well-being while Kathera lay at home, asleep, fighting for hers.

I returned to our house and entered quietly. Kathera's thoughts flitted through me, leading me to feel that she had awakened and was active somewhere inside.

I entered the living room, but she wasn't there.

I walked upstairs to the library, where soft candle-light bounced from the walls, leaving a warm glow emanating from the threshold.

"Kathera?" I stepped into the room and approached her; she sat at the desk at the far end with a large sketch-book cracked open in front of her and a desk lamp bent to shine its piercing fluorescent haze onto the pages.

"Where have you been?" she asked, placing her pencil down and then twisting in her chair to look back at me.

"I took a walk." I approached her.

"Are you all right?"

"Shouldn't I be asking you that?"

She glanced away. "I'll be fine. You don't need to

worry about this." She tucked her wrist down beneath the table to hide the mark from me.

"How can I not worry about you? I did not swear my loyalty to you, only to let a man harm you whilst I stand idly by."

"There are battles you cannot win, Matthaya," she whispered, gazing up at me with sadness in her eyes. "And there are demons I must face alone."

Her words pierced my heart.

Like bubbles rising from the ocean depths, a memory long tucked away came rushing to the surface.

I could not find the words to reply to her just then, because a scar of my own had begun to bleed anew.

Regret. Tragedy. Loss.

I'd faced such demons before—and a battle I could not win.

My face lowered and I turned a wrist over to watch lamplight dance across the mismatched cufflinks on my sleeve. My coat had been altered to accommodate two pairs, though the norm was one on each cuff.

Despite my anger toward Derek, I could relate to Kathera's feelings of grief and her sympathy toward him for the loss. Losing a friend is difficult and the wounds left from their absence never truly heal.

There was a sudden growing sense of urgency in me—a deep desire to unearth a piece of my past with which I still struggled to cope. I took a seat in an adjacent chair. "May I... tell you a story?" I asked, gazing at her.

Kathera likely sensed the grim tone in my voice. She reached back to close her sketchbook and then nodded in reply. There was a glimmer of anticipation in her expression.

My gaze returned to my cufflinks; the shimmer of yellow gold reminded me of events I had buried years ago, and the loss of a friend, whom I struggle to lay to rest even a century after his funeral.

12
MATTHAYA

BY THE year 1887, I'd already been living in the Hounslow district in Greater London, England, for nearly a decade. There, I had taken up work as a night watchman for an antiquities dealer, using the position as a means of networking with art dealers who might help me locate Kathryn's painting. It was my solitary responsibility to secure and upkeep the shop after dark. A place fueled by history was a good fit, and the time spent toiling there was generally pleasant.

In only a few years, the city around me had changed dramatically. I witnessed the fall of gas lighting as it succumbed to the advent of electric street lamps. With technology creeping into commonplace, the overall pace of life, for many, had begun to hasten.

A royal cavalry, known as the 10th Hussars, had been stationed nearby. They were a segment of the British Army under the rule of the Prince of Wales, Edward VII, referred to as the "Prince of Wales's Own" regiment. They made rounds about the city every now and then, though I did not know much else about them. Their flashy navy blue uniforms featured multiple accoutrements and aiguillettes, and a sword hung at their sides as they rode their mounts through the streets, seemingly only to make a spectacle.

One cold winter evening, as frost dusted the cobblestone and a light snowfall began to drift down from the black sea of stars, a commotion outside the shop caught my attention. I left my post, locked the door behind me, and went to investigate. Around the corner, I came upon a decorated soldier caught in a power struggle with his horse. I remained a safe distance away to observe.

"What in God's name!" The man tugged the reins and rapped the horse's hindquarters with a crop. Judging by the elaborate, even excessive decorations on his uniform, this was the captain of the Hussars.

The horse whinnied and shifted its body with great

difficulty and discomfort, snorting and bowing its head repeatedly.

"Come now!" The captain raised his voice and clicked his tongue several times, but the animal refused to respond.

I'd seen such behavior before.

"Pardon me, Sir." I stepped out from the shadows and into the lamplight, holding up my empty hands so that he could see I was unarmed. "May I be of assistance?"

The captain glared at me. "State your name and purpose here, young man." He tried to compose himself, but there was uneasiness in his heavy, tired eyes as he shifted in his saddle.

He had called *me* a "young man," but he appeared to be in his early twenties. The prominent, thick, curled mustache below his nose—a popular style at the time— could not distract from his long face and soft, round features, which gave him a youthful, statuesque complexion.

His jacket was decorated with an array of medals, colorful badges, and several lengths of gold aiguillettes draped across his chest and arms.

"Matthew Stewart," I answered. I'd been going by the pseudonym, at the time—a simple first name, and an inconsequential, absurdly common surname. "At your service."

"What are you doing about at this hour?" The pallid shade of his face and listless expression relayed little emotion, but there were shadows of fatigue around his eyes, as if he'd carried some great burden in his soul. Something, other than the horse, had been tormenting the man for many days.

"I superintend R. Ridley's shop at the corner." I looked off to the side and lowered my head respectfully. "I meant no trouble, Sir."

"What is it you want, then?" he asked, pulling back on the reins again, without avail. His horse's head suddenly jerked downward, pulling the captain forward in the saddle and nearly off the beast's back. Embarrassed, he yanked the reins forcefully, drawing the animal's head back up.

"You are having trouble with your mount," I said, trying to assess the situation. "I have a great deal of experience working with horses and I wish to help."

A look of relief came over him. "Ah, well, that is a fine coincidence, then."

"May I approach to examine him?" I asked.

Animals are naturally apprehensive around vampires, but in winter, their senses are dampened by the frigid cold, and my scent masked by it.

"You may," the captain replied. "He has been acting

strange all evening, refusing to follow direction."

I neared the pair and the horse lifted its head with a start, a frightened look gleaming in the whites of its eyes. But as I raised a hand toward its withers, and spoke soft, comforting words to it, I saw that it was not fear in its expression, but discomfort.

"Could you dismount, please, Captain?" I looked up at him, lifting a hand to request the reins.

The captain came down off his saddle, his heavy boots clacking against the cobblestone, and then moved to stand beside me, watching his horse intently.

"Does he have a name?" I asked, bending to press a hand to the back of the horse's front leg. My fingers moved firmly down across the hair, toward the cannon bone and fetlock.

"Father named him Copenhagen, but I have fondly called him Brandy, for his rich bay coat."

"Brandy is fitting," I replied, lifting the horse's leg to examine the hoof for debris or injury. I did not see anything caught in the shoe, or any broken or missing nails. A notably-sized crack did catch my eye.

"It is quite magnificent in the spring when the sun glints off his back as he is grazing." The tone of the captain's voice had softened to one of concern and kindness. By the sound of it, he cared greatly about this horse.

Which was unfortunate, as the fate of this creature

was dubious.

I grasped onto the bridle and pulled the horse forward gently. "Walk up, Brandy." I clicked my tongue.

But he would not obey. Instead, he seized, and his legs went completely straight and stiff. I had felt swelling in the joints and muscle tissue but hoped that I was mistaken.

"What is it?" the captain asked, glancing over my shoulder. "Has he thrown a shoe?"

"I am afraid not," I replied, standing straight and turning to face him. "I am sorry to say that it appears your dear Brandy has foundered."

The captain's eyes widened. "Foundered!? What does that mean?"

"It is a condition sometimes caused by over-consumption of sweet grass in the spring, but," I shrugged, "seeing that it is now winter, it is likely from..." I tried to say the word without sounding accusatory, "overfeeding." I pointed to Brandy's front legs. "It causes swelling and inflammation in the feet, which make the legs stiff and likely painful to move. There's also a prominent crack in his left front hoof."

The captain stared at me with astonishment. "You can tell all that by *looking* at him?"

"And feeling the swelling in his legs, yes." I nodded. "I was raised on a plantation, where I trained some horses.

I saw many an equine illness during my time there."

The captain raised a gloved hand toward his face and cupped his mouth to hide an anxious trembling lip. "What should I do with him?" he asked, gazing at me with worried eyes. "I can get him the best care possible. Money is no concern."

"I am afraid this may not be a financial dilemma," I said solemnly. My lips pressed thin as I ran a few possible scenarios through my mind. Some offered hope for the creature, while most ended in death. Founder, medically known as "laminitis," is not always fatal, but the horse can suffer complications for a lifetime, complications often 'treated' with euthanasia, at the time.

"Some will recommend he be put down," I started. The captain's brow rose with disbelief and his jaw dropped. The sorrow in his eyes made me reconsider my diagnosis. "But," I continued, scratching Brandy behind his ears, "I believe that should be reserved only for when Brandy, too, has lost hope. He has a soldier's heart, no doubt. He may be able to live a quiet, peaceful life with the proper care, though his days of service to the king are over."

I took a step back.

"Oh, Brandy," the captain whispered, pressing his forehead to Brandy's muzzle. The horse pushed back gently and affectionately. "Father will not take you away, my friend," the captain said, his voice breaking.

He heaved a breath.

I was certain I was not supposed to have heard his comment, but my sensitive ears did, and it led me to wonder who the man's father was.

"You appear too young to be so knowledgeable," he said, "but I thank you for your educated evaluation; I will have him seen again in the morning and will do whatever I can for him. What does my family owe you for your time?"

I raised a flattened hand and shook my head. "You owe me nothing."

Skepticism wrinkled his brow. "I have not met a man who would do work for no pay."

"I work because it is a welcome respite from boredom," I replied, truthfully.

"Are you a nobleman, then?"

"No."

"Then, why?"

I glanced down the street toward the corner from whence I'd come. "I should be going, Sir. Pardon me, but I cannot leave the shop unattended." I bowed my head and turned to leave.

"Sir Stewart, wait!" He pulled Brandy's reins, but the horse stalled, his front legs locking up again. Then he looped them over the saddle and walked briskly after me. "Please, wait."

I paused and turned toward him.

"I apologize if I appeared to be prying. I was only curious about you since you seem so worldly and... *I* have so very much to learn. My father has sent me all over the country and the world, but none of those ventures granted me any respite from my own boredom. You, though... you have the aura of a well-traveled soul. What is it that keeps you moving forward?"

"It is true that I have traveled much and lived in many places. It is also true that I have never found a place I consider to be my home."

"Is that so?" He narrowed his eyes. "Well, if you tire of your position here, would you have any interest in becoming a caretaker for my horse?"

Leave my position at the antiquity shop and risk losing track of Kathryn's painting?

"I can give you time to think about it," the captain continued, after my moment of hesitation.

It wasn't time I needed, just then. I preferred to keep my head down and stay amongst the common folk. But I saw something in his troubled eyes that reminded me of myself, and it made me reconsider his request.

I also knew that if anyone else were to take hold of his gelding, they'd put him down in an instant, regardless of the captain's sentiments. Founder was typically an acute illness that would flare up if not treated stringently and proactively. His horse could suffer bouts of stiffness and pain—days when he would be unwilling to be ridden at all.

"How much do you want to keep that horse?" I asked, glancing at the poor creature standing listlessly in the distance.

"Keep him? You say that as though his grave has already been prepared."

"In the eyes of some, it has. I have not met many veterinarians who would suggest otherwise."

"Oh..." He glanced back at his horse. "Well, I will not allow him to be put down, unless there remains no other choice. He's a fine horse and fair-mannered. Calm. Listens well."

"Keeping him will require careful feeding and attention," I informed him. "He could live comfortably, perhaps, but he should be retired from this work."

He looked off to the side. "I understand what it means to suffer in the line of duty."

I hadn't quite understood what he'd meant. Perhaps he, too, endured some chronic disease.

He cleared his throat again and tried to smile, his thick, curled mustache masking the grin. "I will ask you again, Sir, would you accept a position with me as the caretaker of my horse? My family will pay you substantially—double. No. Triple whatever that shop owner is giving you now for the petty work he has put you to.”

“I do not consider my work to be petty,” I retorted, put off by the suggestion, though I didn't think he had meant it maliciously. “But, I do agree it is not a prestigious job. I must ask a question of you, however. Why would you do such a thing for me? You do not even know me. How do you know you can trust me?”

“Your eyes tell a great deal about you,” he said firmly, staring back at me. “You say you work to escape boredom and that money is not a matter that concerns you… but I see a man who has faced many perils and one who carries many burdens. We have much in common in that regard. You have the air of a man who can be trusted.”

I thought on it, studying him intently as I contemplated his offer. I could go back to seeking out Kathryn's painting as soon as the captain's horse recovered enough to be cared for by another. Or maybe the connection could assist me in my search.

“I must keep certain hours, for *personal* reasons,” I said flatly.

He tipped his head. “You may come and go as you wish.”

I paused to assure myself that I was making the right decision. “Then I accept your proposition.” We shared a hearty handshake.

Without releasing his hand, I looked into his pale

blue eyes and asked, "Who shall I be working for?"

⳾ ⳾

I had been employed, and befriended, by His Royal Highness Prince Albert Victor Christian Edward of Wales, soon to be Duke of Clarence and Avondale, next in line for the British throne, after his father, Edward VII, and grandmother, Queen Victoria.

Or as his close friends and supporters lovingly called him, Eddy.

Eddy was a composed, sympathetic man, who tried to follow his heart and aspirations, even as the world conspired against him. His father sent him on many military tours in an effort to toughen up the future king, but all it did was make Eddy miserable while feeding the flames of his critics. Rumors of unsavory things—such as having personal investments in an illegal brothel—spread like wildfire throughout the people. I was in no position to help him during the day, but under the cover of night, I could threaten some accusers. This allowed me to snuff out many of the lies, but never them all. Being in the public eye had many downsides for his fragile character.

Despite my best efforts, social criticism caused him constant grief, and with complications of Brandy's condition eventually forcing the prince to face the worst, he fell into despair.

Though his father was not fond of me, Queen Victoria appointed me as Eddy's official advisor. I willingly accepted the position, out of fear that declining it would plunge my friend into darkness blacker than my own. It was her belief that my presence gave him the spark of courage he so desperately needed during his struggle with depression and the media.

But my friendship could not protect him from it all. Each time I rescued him from the edge of despair, the undertow would drag him down again.

On his family's demand, he became engaged, while very much in love with another woman—one he could not have because of their religious differences. Still, their love flourished in letters and brief meetings over the years I'd accompanied him. I was an accomplice in these secret meetings and I helped hide the letters in which he poured out his heart to her.

Perhaps I should not have done such a thing. Perhaps I should have let his family force him to marry another, or have even encouraged him to. But his angst resonated with me, because I know the pain of what it is to love someone while the universe conspires against you.

He and I did have much in common; though our upbringings were very different, our souls carried similar grievances. This made the endeavor to help him a deeply personal one, and it eventually led to my revealing the truth of who, and *what*, I was…

It was late one night. I had closed myself off in a room at the far end of Eddy's family's manor, as I always did when I had to indulge in blood to soothe the hunger.

Usually, no one bothered me after dark.

I heard heavy footsteps up the stairs, nearing my room.

"Matthew?" Eddy called out, his speech slurred and hoarse. "Matthew, we must speak."

I remained silent, hoping he'd assume I was asleep.

But he knew me better.

He pounded on the door. The scent of alcohol wafted into my room.

He wasn't much of a drinker… except… on occasion.

"Matthew!"

A female servant came to his aid. "My Lord, you'll wake the household. Come. Let's take you back to your room and—"

"I must speak to my friend!" I heard a scuffle and then the pounding continued. The clumsy, heavy footsteps rattled me and I was forced to set my bottle of blood on the side table.

I hurried to the door and flung it open. "Let him be," I said, glaring at the servant. "I will see to it that he is cared for."

The petite old woman cowered and backed away, tipping her head while nervously replying, "Yes. Yes."

She'd always been intimidated by me.

I reached out to wrap an arm around Eddy's shoulders to support his drunken weight as I turned him toward my room.

"Come, Eddy. Let us speak."

"The Prime Minister will not sanction it," he said, hanging over the arm of the chair. "And my love's father will not allow her to convert. The dear Queen has done all she can to help, but the damned law simply will not allow a Roman Catholic into the royal family. Even as my heart burns only for Hélène, the law will not grant me such a love marriage." Eddy's reddening eyes glistened with the threat of tears. "*I* do not wish to be king. I tried to denounce the throne, but—"

"You did what?"

"I told Father I would relinquish my title and leave the throne to my brother, but it was not enough. Even the Pope conspires against us, stealing away from me the only joy I have ever found." He fell back in the chair and dropped his face into his hands. "Why? Why am I here? I wish to be dead and done with it all."

Impeded by a long list of ridiculous formalities and

political and religious differences, his dream of marrying the French princess of Orléans would never come to fruition.

I knew exactly what it was to be ensnared by forbidden love.

"I am sorry those around you do not see your pain or heed your desires. The world is not always fair and—"

"Is that wine?" Eddy lunged from the chair toward the bottle of blood on the table across from him. "Let me have it." He flailed an arm and wrapped his fingers around the neck. "Damn it, Matthew. I... am... the son of..."

"No!" I growled, wrestling it from his hands.

"Your eyes!?" He stared at me, his mouth agape. "What is wrong with your eyes?" Eddy stiffened in the chair. "I cannot possibly be *that* drunk that I would hallucinate."

I grasped the bottle firmly and brought it close to my chest, realizing now that my eyes must have flickered with light.

I was both hungry and worried about him accidentally consuming the blood.

But most of all, I was tired of keeping the secret from a friend.

"Matthew?" Eddy tipped his head to the side. He seemed sober now, somehow, though he surely wasn't. "What is it? You can trust me, you know."

"You cannot have this," I said gruffly, holding the bottle up and out of his reach.

"What is it?"

I poured a small amount into my palm and revealed it to him. His eyes widened, but he did not recoil.

"Blood?" His gaze went from my palm to my eyes. "Are you an alchemist? What do you use it for?"

I tipped my head back and took a long swig from the bottle, feeling relief flow through my body as the blood washed down my throat.

Our eyes met again and I gestured toward Kathryn's painting, which now sat prominently above the fireplace of my room. Eddy's connections had helped me locate and procure it, further solidifying my desire to help him and remain his companion.

"There are things I must tell you, my friend," I began. "That girl in the painting..."

He glanced up at it and wiped tears from his cheeks.

"She was not one of my distant relatives. She was the woman I loved but could not have."

He gasped. "She was your Hélène?" he uttered in disbelief.

"Yes."

"But... how? That painting is nearly three hundred years old." He stared inquisitively at the bottle. "Does that prolong your life?"

"In a way." I took another drink. "But not without an unfortunate cost." The light in my eyes flared again and I bared my teeth enough for him to easily see the fangs which were usually subtly hidden. Any other human may have run screaming into the night after I revealed the supernatural glimmer in my eyes, but not Eddy.

He slid off his chair and approached me, reaching out to place a hand on my shoulder. "Matthew..."

"Matthaya," I corrected him.

"Matthaya?" He repeated my name softly, with admiration. "There is surely greatness in that name. I had a feeling there was more to you." He smiled thoughtfully at me. "Matthaya," he said, pressing his fingers against my shoulder. "I will not question your motives or your past, as you have never questioned mine. You have stood beside me through all the accusations and hardships I have faced these past few years and I am honored for your trust in me. You are but one thing to me: a true friend."

His words surprised me; they left me speechless. I had never known another man to hold such understanding and love in his heart—especially toward a creature like myself. But Eddy was good-hearted, despite the ill intentions of so many around him. He never let it corrupt him.

"We are brothers in our losses, then," he continued, patting me on the shoulder. "And no other man will know my pain better than you, Matthaya."

The way my name slid off his tongue with respect and appreciation made my burdens seem lighter. It had been years since someone had called me by my real name, for I had been afraid to reveal it after everything that had happened in my past. But he accepted me for who I was.

For *what* I was.

Without question.

℘ ℭ

It was the dawn of the year 1892, and on his 28th birthday, Eddy (now the Duke of Clarence and Avondale) urgently requested my presence in his drawing room.

"Come see what the Queen has gifted me." He sat near the fireplace with a heavy wool blanket draped over his legs. In his lap lay an intricately carved wooden box inlaid with ivory and lapis. He twisted slowly in his chair to look back at me. "Turn the light on, will you?" he asked, and gestured for me to come closer.

I turned the knob on the wall and the electric lights buzzed to life, flooding the room with a bright, sunny glow that trumped the soft amber of the crackling fire. It also illuminated his face, forcing me to look upon the pallid, sunken skin barely clinging to the bones of his once round cheeks.

"I cannot tell you how much that sound pleases me,"

he said in a weak but enthusiastic tone, gazing with tired eyes at the nearby lamp on the wall beside him. "I am blessed to live in an era of change and wonder."

"As am I," I replied, approaching the side of his chair and looking over his shoulder at the box.

"I must show you my gift," he said, lifting the lid. Light reflected upon the things, sending a glint of metal sparkling back at us. Inside the box were two pairs of solid gold cufflinks set upon a majestic backdrop of sapphire-colored velvet.

"Are these not the most magnificent pieces you have ever seen?" he asked, raising the box toward me with shaky hands. "The Queen commissioned them for me from a smith in Essex."

"They are exquisite," I replied.

Queen Victoria loved Eddy and often gave him extravagant, sometimes useless, gifts to show her affection, but the cufflinks exhibited masterful craftsmanship and thought. I leaned down to examine them more closely.

"Here." Eddy handed the box to me, smiling with such delight that I thought his heart might burst.

I wrapped both hands gingerly around the box and brought it toward my face. The two pairs of cufflinks were different, but similar in design. Each of them had been engraved with a simple, elegant pattern reminiscent of the aiguillettes decorating the royal family's attire. They were diamond-shaped—an unusual choice for such a piece of jewelry—but it also made them distinct and rare in appearance. Befitting of a future king.

"Do you like them?" he asked, straining to smile. "Do you like them as much as I do?"

I chuckled softly and handed the box back to him. "Yes. They are wonderful."

"Then let us share them." His frail fingers began working them free from the velvet backing.

I tipped my head, came around to the front of his chair, and then knelt. "My friend, there is no need for you to give such a gift to me. I am not deserving of it."

"Nonsense, Matthaya." The pale duke leaned forward in his chair and looked me square in the eye. "You have changed me for the better, man. Because of you, I have a sharper sense of judgment and fairness than ever before. You are the reason I chose to not only accept the position as Viceroy of Ireland, but also to embrace that power in an effort to better the relationship between our two homelands. Giving you these would be the absolute least I could possibly do to repay you for the huge kindness and wisdom you have bestowed upon me."

He finally pried out two matching cufflinks. "Here," he said, reaching for my hand. I raised it to his lap and he nestled the two gold pieces within my palm with his frigid fingers. I grasped them carefully.

"Thank you," I said softly, trying my best to smile gratefully at Eddy. "I will keep them with me always."

"No," he added, clutching onto my hand with both of his. "Thank *you*." Then he released me and polished the other pair of cufflinks with his fingertips, gazing upon them with great satisfaction and joy. "You have taught me that one man's suffering is not wholly his own, and that we all share roles in this human experience. And you have given me reason to believe that my heart is right, and that love cannot be forced by the hand of another."

A peaceful few moments passed and then his smile began to fade and his face wrinkled with discomfort. He coughed and crumpled over in his seat, heaving for air.

"Eddy?" I grasped his shoulder. He was having another fit. "Eddy, are you all right?"

He cleared his throat and straightened back up in his seat, slowly. "Yes. I am fine." He gasped and his lungs wheezed. "I despise this weather," he said. "The cold, damp nature of this foul place will be the death of me." He tried to laugh, but a coughing fit seized him again.

13

MATTHAYA

"THAT PLACE *was* the death of him," I said to Kathera. "He died of pneumonia a few days later." I reached down my sleeve to slide my thumb across one of the gold cufflinks Eddy had gifted me over a century ago.

"I'm so sorry," she replied, reaching out to caress my hand.

"On his deathbed, moments before I was escorted out of the room, he had turned to me and uttered, 'Remember me, and we shall both live forever.'

"His death shocked us all. He was so young, and—with my council—had finally begun to find courage and purpose in his life. Today, he is a forgotten prince, over-shadowed by the legacy of his younger brother, King George V."

"That's terrible," Kathera said softly. "Britain's lost king. What happened to the princess he wanted to marry?"

"She had written him a letter several months prior, asking him to do his royal duty and forget her. He was engaged to another woman only four months after that. Then he died less than a month later. I believe his broken heart left him weak, allowing pneumonia to easily snatch him from the earth."

"It was hard on you, wasn't it?" Kathera asked.

"Very." I looked into her azure eyes. "The loss weighed heavily on my heart then and continues to now. I had not befriended another, until *you* entered my life."

"I hope you can still pay your respects," she said. "Where was he buried?"

"Eddy's mother kept his room and turned it into a shrine, and then commissioned an extravagant tomb for his final resting place in St. George's Chapel in Windsor, tucked away down a corridor most will never visit. It's one of the most profound dedications I've ever seen. A grand angel kneels weeping at the head of it, a crown held aloft in her hands, and a beautiful but tragic sculpture of Eddy in his full dress uniform, recumbent, as if he'd fallen asleep right atop the tomb and been turned to stone. It broke my heart to view it in all its glory. The details and craftsmanship were clearly meant to honor him, but looking upon it reminded me of the frailty of us all. It reminded me, yet again, that I could never have friends."

My jaw tightened and I growled beneath my breath.

"What is it?" Kathera leaned closer, pressing her fingertips against my arm.

"Bad memories," I replied, glancing at her again. "I'm sorry to bore you with details, but I have never told another about these things, and thus they have eaten at me for years."

"I am happy to hear the story, and I'm grateful to learn more about you," she added. "Please, go on. I'm here to listen."

"Eddy couldn't rest, not even in death. The media planted and fueled a theory that he had been the one responsible for the gruesome murders made by Jack the Ripper. Pure ridiculousness, but the public hungered for a good story, especially when there was no one around to deny it." I shook my head angrily. "Eddy was nowhere near London at the time of those murders, and I would know because *I* was with him then. But the accusations took wing years after his death, and I was forced to turn a blind eye until historians finally cleared his name. It infuriated me, though, to be unable to defend my friend's honor. At least he can rest in peace now."

I reached into a flap of my jacket, tucking my fingers into the small breast pocket hidden inside. "I never showed you this," I said, withdrawing a carte de visite—a small black and white albumin photograph taken in 1890. It had turned a shade of beige and taken on an unpleasant bit of foxing near the edges of the mounting frame, but it was in generally good condition.

"Eddy once asked me to take a photograph with him. He told me he'd wanted it as a reminder that all men exist with reason, and to give him courage and strength in times of uncertainty.

"I had declined at the time, but my rejection brought a great deal of sorrow to him, so I changed my mind and honored his request, under the condition that only two copies be made. One—to be buried with him. The other— to be buried with me."

"Did Eddy ever ask you to explain exactly what you are? He obviously knew something was different, especially when he found you with the bottle of blood."

"He knew I had been alive for many years beyond a normal human lifespan, and that I was not like other men. He accepted me as that."

Kathera rested her head on my shoulder. "It's strange seeing such an old photo of you. You look nearly the same, just a little younger." She traced a finger across the bottom of the photograph. It showed Eddy in a dress uniform sitting on a carved throne with me standing beside him. They did not tell you, or wish for you, to smile back then, and it made the shadows of grief on both our faces more apparent.

"I'd been wondering why your cufflinks didn't match," Kathera said. She squinted and leaned closer to the photograph. Then she brought a hand up to her collarbone and clasped the golden cross pendant hanging there.

I had been wearing the cross in the photo, though it was hardly noticeable, and it could be seen peeking out just below my collar, from the edge of my necktie.

"Thank you for sharing that story with me," Kathera added, looking over at me. "I understand you're trying to help me cope with my feelings about Derek, but Prince Eddy's death wasn't your fault. You didn't cause his illness, nor could you have saved him from it."

But the thought kept rising in my mind: had I known I was a Sire back then, then perhaps I—

"Would you have wanted that responsibility?" Kathera asked, gazing at me after having read my mind.

"No." The answer came to me without hesitation. "But, at the time, I may have thought differently. Unfortunately, regret, too, is immortal. It was only a fleeting few years of friendship, but his death took a piece of my own soul to the grave. I had not felt so empty since losing Kathryn."

"Be at peace with the time that you had with him," she said. "Know that you gave him friendship and courage. You believed in him when others didn't."

"Do you regret it?" I asked, reaching for her hand. "Do you regret what I did to you?"

"No." She shook her head, and I could feel in my blood that she spoke truth. "The life I was trapped in before you came, was no life at all. And while I know this one has its challenges, I have you. Even if I am to continue battling nightmares, you will be here when I wake." She scooted closer, forked her fingers through my hair, and then kissed me. "I will never regret being with you," she whispered.

14

KATHERA

THE SCENT of mustiness and decay made my nose wrinkle. I opened my eyes to find myself sitting in a dirty, decrepit room with ugly, off-white drywall riddled with holes. Broken picture frames and torn canvases lay on the ground, and remnants of plaster dust and strips of shredded wallpaper littered the floor.

My shoulders were bare; shreds of clothing scarcely covered me: a sleeveless torn crop top, cut embarrassingly high, and a grungy, meager denim skirt with threads spiraling down from all sides of the hem—hardly covering my thighs.

Vintage erotic art cluttered the wall opposite me, roughly-colored, distasteful, and some, even gruesome. Glancing over them nauseated me—women who'd been gagged, chained, or tied to furniture... like prisoners.

Derek had better taste than this.

I'd seen some bad art in the tattoo industry and had been asked to do some offensive designs, but I had no tolerance for people who took pleasure in images with gross violent natures.

Dingy window curtains fluttered nearby and I turned toward them as a faint breeze squeezed in through a crack in the clouded window. It appeared to be daytime, but such a thick layer of greasy haze covered the window that very little light shone through.

Filthy place.

I looked around the uncomfortably small room. A battered writing desk with only three legs had been shoved into one of the corners with no chair in sight. No door, either.

Where was I? I came to my feet and began searching for a way out. There were no vents, no ceiling tiles, nothing, only a sad excuse for a window and no mechanism by which it could be opened. I shoved my hands against the warm glass and pried my fingers into the frame, but it didn't budge. It must have been two inches thick, as it didn't make a sound when I slammed my shoulder against it.

A heavy thud vibrated through the floor and I veered around.

There was the missing chair, with Derek upon it. He sat on it the wrong way—his characteristic preference—legs straddled over the seat and his forearms resting across the craggy wooden back.

"Hi again," he said, an intense glare centered on me and anticipation in his smile.

My knees felt heavy, as if my blood had pooled in the lower half of my body, and I could no longer feel my fingers beyond a strange tingling.

"What do you want?" I tried to cross my arms in an effort to cover my bare midriff, but my body wouldn't comply. All I could do was turn my head slightly to the side and avoid eye contact with him.

"Just you," he replied, his toothy grin revealing no vampire fangs this time. "Come here," he said, curling a finger inward as he leaned over the back of the chair.

"No." I imagined my hands curling into fists, and my knees locking, but they wouldn't. An invisible force made me take a step toward him, my legs moving without my consent.

Fear crushed me.

I had lost control over my body, even as my mind fought to regain it. "Don't do this to me," I managed to speak. "Please."

At least I could still talk.

"Oh, I'm not gonna *make* you do anything," he said. His callous laugh made the hairs on the back of my neck stand and my heart thump against my ribcage.

He gestured for me to come closer, and I did, even though I strained to try to stop my feet from moving. I wanted to turn and run, anywhere, as long as it was away from him and that repulsive place.

But my body continued to act against my will. I wanted to fight it—I tried to stop myself from approaching him, but my consciousness began slipping from my grasp, my ability to control my own movements driven back, trapping me inside a body that would no longer obey.

Within moments, I was inches from where he sat, poised in a strange, suggestive stance, with a hand set upon my hip and my back curved into an uncomfortable pose.

"I'd never force myself on you," he said. "What the hell kind of man would I be if I did that? Not yours, right?" A broad, cruel smirk twisted on his lips. "I'm just gonna let you be you."

The man sitting before me was not the Derek that I once knew.

I took another step closer.

Stop!

I was detached, a host watching through the eyes of a vessel she could no longer control.

My hands lifted up over my head and my head fell back, my torso contorting as my hips began to sashay to a rhythm I couldn't hear—some hypnotic beat pounding through my bones and making me twist and move in ways I'd never moved. I stroked my hands down my sides, sliding up and down my hips and chest, bending and moving with graceful serpent-like form. I was a zombie partaking in a provocative dance, unable to stop my limbs and hands from moving and touching my body sensually.

That's when Derek stood from the chair and came up beside me, devouring me with black eyes.

A cry for help erupted in my mind but never escaped my lips, nor shaped my face. The next thing I knew, I was writhing down his side, my hair catching on the wrinkles of his clothing as I moved in ways that made my stomach churn. He clasped onto my hips, tugging me in close to his chest so the curves of my body were unnervingly flush against his.

The friction of our bodies rubbing together incited a deep, visceral sense of violation and vulnerability; I shuddered and flinched. Still, nothing manifested on the outside, and the skittering thoughts were trapped in the prison behind my eyes.

Derek's fingertips slid past my waist, to my thighs, then just beneath the hem of my skirt, where they bunched the fabric up toward my hips and pressed against my naked leg.

Our bodies swayed in rhythm to a beat only he could hear, as his desires controlled me like a puppet.

He took a deep breath, the airy sound close to my ear, and then exhaled against the back of my neck. "I want you," he whispered. Our bodies nearly tangled together already, his lust raged. His hands glided up and down my sides, traversing parts of my flesh no one should touch without permission.

His need for me spun out of control and those cravings pushed my personal choices to take a backseat to his own corrupt desires, my shell of a body doing only what *he* willed, while I watched in terror through a two-way mirror.

He latched on to my hand and spun me to face him, forcing me to lock eyes with him again. A hand crept down to the bare skin at the small of my back, and when he pulled me in close, our bodies touched in places only lovers should.

Let me go. Please!

My arms wouldn't force him back. My legs wouldn't take me away. I didn't want to be this close, but I couldn't stop enticing him to carry on with his vile desires. My body consented to the madness *against my will.*

This isn't you, Derek.

The words never made it past my lips.

I'd have trembled and cried out if I could have. My eyes would have welled with tears and my lungs would have quaked with each unwanted stroke of his fingers down my ribs. A muffled moan of displeasure vibrated in my throat—a single, audible blip I'd been able to force through the barrier of his control, but it wasn't enough to stop him.

I imagined letting out a scream, forcing him back, and then scrambling to escape.

When he kissed the side of my neck and grazed my throat with his tongue, I imagined myself holding my breath and clenching my teeth in rebellion, but instead, I dropped my head back. I wanted to fight back, but my body only encouraged him to continue, responding to the uninvited advances with subtle sighs of pleasure and flitting, eager breaths. His teeth made shallow marks along my neck and the heat of his exhalations made me lightheaded.

Please... No.

I wanted to wake up. I wanted it all to go away.

Long ago, I'd wanted him once. I'd thought about it, at least.

But...

I was married now, and...

I didn't want him to...

Stop! Stop touching me!

But he wouldn't.

He pulled the shoulder of my ragged shirt down, exposing my collarbone and cleavage, and then he leaned down to kiss me there. The fabric stretched until it tore, splitting across my chest and sliding away until it left me raw and exposed. I wanted to cover myself. At least, I tried.

I thought he might reach for my skirt next, but instead, *I* pressed my hands onto his shoulders and we knelt together on the floor.

The anger and sickness in my mind intensified while my fingers worked fervently to unbutton his shirt even as I recoiled in the dark corners of my consciousness, unable to turn away. Unable to shut my eyes.

Guilt rattled me as I took hold of the flaps of his shirt and pushed him onto the dirty floor so that I could straddle his waist and caress my hands over his taut, sweaty chest.

Shame filled me as I came down to kiss him, my naked skin colliding with his. I used one hand to prop myself up, and my other to deftly unclasp his belt.

No. No. No!

I revolted in my mind, to no avail. Every ravenous

desire of *his* body and mind manipulated and controlled me. Imprisoned behind a mask of my own free will, I was forced to seduce him.

15

KATHERA

I AWOKE famished, with a whirlwind of anxiety surging through my veins, flooding me with sensations of fear and nearby threats. Pain resonated in my abdomen and I curled into a fetal position, pulling my knees to my belly.

Why am I hurting?

Matthaya had assured me numerous times that we couldn't experience pain, but pain was very much what I was experiencing, yet again. I turned my wrist over to look at the bite mark—still faded purple and bruised. Hairline forks of black and gray radiated beneath the skin. I grimaced, closed my eyes, and tucked my arm back under the blanket.

"How long do you expect me to allow this to go on?" Matthaya asked.

He stood in the doorway, leaning on the frame, his vivid green eyes locked on me. I pushed onto my back and fought to sit up, clenching my teeth as the pain intensified.

"How long, Kathera?" he asked, approaching the bedside and gazing down at me. Patience shaped his face, but anger raged behind the quiet façade.

"He'll stop," I said, keeping my arm hidden from view. "I know he will." I broke eye contact and didn't continue; no words could explain why I didn't want my husband to retaliate.

In his mind, I was the victim. In mine, it was Derek's warped sense of justice carrying out the sentence for my crimes. Or, at least, the crimes he perceived I had committed toward him.

"I will not stand by and watch you be tortured," he said, kneeling at the edge of the bed. "Please tell me what to do to help you."

I didn't know what he could do.

He pressed his lips thin. "If you will not tell me, then at least tell me what he's done to you. You are radiating pain, and you should not be. I can't seem to reach you while you sleep, but now that you're awake, I—"

Glimpses of the nightmare replayed and I tried to snuff out the visions.

But Matthaya caught them instantly. His brow crinkled as he bit down and growled, a radiant verdant glow sparking in his eyes. "He... *raped* you!"

"Only in my mind," I replied swiftly.

"How dare you defend him," he hissed. "How dare you ignore the obscenities he's forced upon you!"

"I'm not *ignoring* his actions," I whispered, ashamed of my desire to defend him still. "Once he has this out of his system, he'll stop. He'll leave me alone. He'll leave *us* alone."

"He will leave us alone if I *kill* him." Matthaya stood forcefully and bared his fangs.

"No!"

His eyes glinted toxic green. He stepped closer to me and bent down to eye level. "Give me one good reason why I shouldn't defend you. One reason why I shouldn't put an end to him for what he's done. Tell me. I. Must. Know."

I looked up into his eyes and frowned, the pain slowly dissipating from my abdomen. The bright rage firing in his irises intimidated me.

He was right to be angry.

He was right to want to protect me.

And I was a fool for asking him to not. What Derek

was doing to me was wrong, and yet...

"I'm not proud of how I treated him back then, nor will I ever be free of the guilt of his death and corruption by Ve'tani, but I can't ignore the truth behind why I stayed with him for so long. I cared about Derek, and I abused his trust by hanging on to you as if all he'd done had meant nothing to me. But that wasn't true. It wasn't true at all.

"I kept telling myself I couldn't love him, until I believed it. But a few months after you left, there was a moment when we were together and, for one second, I stopped thinking about you and I started thinking about *us*.

"Derek granted me sanctuary and freedom from the pain of you walking away from me. He cared for me, and he treated me with so much goodness and respect when I didn't deserve his kindness."

"But you told me you didn't want to marry him," Matthaya said.

"Maybe I didn't, but I didn't want him to die, either. Maybe it wasn't love, but I felt something for him."

I eased up from the bed, bracing myself for any sudden pain, but it didn't strike. Then I looked into Matthaya's eyes and said, "I know it's difficult to understand—seeing what he's become—but I couldn't live with myself if I let him die a second time."

Matthaya shifted his weight and looked off to the side, his mind toiling with the myriad of emotional memories darting through my mind and echoing across his.

"You feel some gratitude toward him for what he did for you," he said, "and you are also grappling with the regret of his mortal death. I understand your desire to bargain for his life with your feelings." He gracefully took my chin between his thumb and index finger and tipped my face up; his fierce, concerned look ensnared me. "But as your husband, it is my obligation to protect you, and to see to it that you are free from unnecessary strife."

His thumb pressed against my chin. "I will put this aside, *for now*. Only because you have begged me to, and because I respect your wishes, though they do not bring me any comfort. But, if he touches you again—in your mind or otherwise—I *will* end him."

The thought of Matthaya tearing Derek apart roused an ache in my heart I could not quell.

"Kathera?" His voice softened and he released my chin to stroke the back of his hand across my cheek. "You must consider my feelings, too. I have suffered trying to save those whom I cared about, and the past nips at my heels even today."

Losing Kathryn when he was younger had left a deep scar in his soul, as did losing Eddy to a premature end.

Derek, too, was a scar—a tattoo on my soul, and a

burden I'd carry forever.

I lifted a hand toward my collarbone and I clasped onto the cross pendant hanging from my neck. "We all have old wounds," I said. "I never meant to reopen yours, nor have I ever wished to see you in pain." I dropped the gold charm back against my skin. "I'm sorry, Matthaya."

"What's done is done. Do not apologize for the past. I am not the Sire Ve'tani is, and I will not attempt to control you. You are mine, but you are not my property."

I smiled at him and reached up to swipe his hair away from his brow. He quickly grabbed my hand and stopped it where it was, then proceeded to slowly bring it down to his cheek, where he pressed my palm against his skin and closed his eyes.

"I would not wish this life upon anyone," he said, his eyes remaining shut. "Not you. Not Derek."

A shred of ache rippled through me, resonating from him, even as his face did not show it. "Please know that this is how I feel," he added, resting some weight against my cupped hand.

I began to wonder if Matthaya's desire to end Derek's life was not crafted from vengeance, but mercy.

16

MATTHAYA

KATHERA HAD asked me not to pursue Derek for his deeds against her, but I'd be damned if I'd allow him to continue torturing her.

The brief glimpse of what he'd done to her drained every last ounce of patience from me. It didn't matter that it was only in her mind. It mattered that he had forced himself on her and marred her physical body with phantom pain she should not have been able to experience.

My clenched fist began to draw blood.

I relaxed my tightly curled fingers so as to not alert

Kathera of my ruminating.

I told her I would leave it alone. For now.

She was in her study, reading a book, and I remained in the living room in an attempt to hide my culminating anger. I *had* told her I would let it go, but the truth was that I could not.

The man claiming to have loved the woman I married dared to burrow into her mind and strip her of her most intimate, sacred possession. Whether physical or psychological, the abuse and trauma *did* occur.

How had he changed so drastically from the man she knew before? I'd seen a hint of darkness in his eyes the day I decided to leave Kathera with him. At the time, I'd thought it was rivalry and past experiences fueling that fire, but now I began to consider the fact that he may have been hiding a greater evil all along.

But that could also be an unfair assumption.

Even I have done horrible things because of the disease and the way it corrupted my mind in the beginning stages. And we all harbor our tragedies when we die. We all fume with regret and anger. Even sorrow.

Derek didn't know where or how to focus his stagnate feelings, and Ve'tani's ill intentions likely weren't helping the situation. She could have taken him far from here and allowed him to flourish in a new place, free of his past.

But she did not.

I closed my eyes and tried to clear my mind of it all.

Someone's watchful gaze had fallen upon me. I looked up at Kathryn's painting—at the subtle grin that once comforted me, and at the inquisitive, almost judgmental expression staring back.

Did I see disappointment on her face now? Or was my guilty conscience playing tricks on me?

I glanced at the gold cufflink on my sleeve; Eddy had helped me procure her painting. In less than five years of working together, he had helped me locate what I couldn't find in nearly two hundred on my own. Without him and his connections, I may have been searching for another century or more.

There were times before then when I would find myself in utter dismay, doubting the possibility that I would ever actually find the rare artifact of my past. But when doubt clouded my perception, I busied myself with other things—with living a life around others, even as I despised human company. My condition did not allow me to make friends easily (or to keep them for long), and the needs of vampirism complicated that with my constant thirst for human blood.

Kathera had begun researching the origins of my emerald ring and the dragon emblems around the setting. Working at the antiquities shop had taught me about the antiques trade, but I would need someone with knowl-edge of the very early 17th century to help me learn more about the ring I'd been carrying since childhood.

I glanced over at Kathera's laptop. She was upstairs getting ready to leave for the shop and had left her notes on the kitchen counter.

She'd been doing a lot of research between working with clients and resting her mind, and had a notebook full of things she'd discovered. I went over to her work-space and flipped open the cover of the notebook. Between scribbled website addresses and the names of people of interest were tiny doodles—characteristic of her style of note-taking.

I skimmed a few pages and then came across a list of names and phone numbers where one name had been underlined several times and starred heavily.

"Dr. Eleanor Henson," it read, followed by a phone number with an area code very different from ours.

A quick internet search informed me that Dr. Henson was a professor of history, had a doctorate in historical studies with a focus on pre-18th century Ireland, and that she had written several books on the British Occupation.

Kathera must have done a great deal of research to have found an expert in such a specific vein of history.

I spun my emerald ring around my finger and won-dered if she had reached out to the doctor yet.

"You can call her, if you'd like," Kathera spoke, descending from the stairwell.

I turned toward her.

"We've been corresponding via email, but hoping to arrange a way to sit and talk in person."

"In person?" From what I'd briefly learned about the doctor, she was a professor at a university in British Columbia. She lived nearly on the other side of the continent.

Kathera stepped down off the final stair and walked over to me. "Yes. I sent photos of your ring to her, as well as Kathryn's painting, and she said she'd be willing to fly down here to authenticate them and have a conversation with us."

Apprehension began to flood my body. "That painting *is* authentic."

"I hadn't mentioned any of this yet," Kathera added, "because I knew it might be difficult for you. But, if you want to speak with her yourself, first, maybe that would ease your mind."

"I won't allow a stranger to touch Kathryn's painting." I looked down at my hand. "Or my ring." I had learned much about authenticating artifacts while working at the antiquities shop before I'd met Eddy. "How do you know she'll be able to tell anything else by seeing these in person?"

"I don't, but she has a list of accolades that indicate she's our best chance. Considering she offered to pay her own way here just to take a look must mean something."

Or that my pieces were invaluable.

"Speak with her, please," Kathera added. "I know you're not trusting of new people, but I feel like she may be able to help you—*us*—learn more about who we are."

"Then let her come."

Kathera seemed surprised by my response and gazed at me inquisitively.

"You trust that she can help us, so I trust that you are right," I said. "Have her make arrangements. We can change things around the house so that it will not seem out of place, and it should be fine."

"Are you sure you're comfortable with that?"

"I will be," I replied. "Offer to pay for her trip and lodging, as well. I understand it will be a lengthy flight for her."

Kathera smiled. "Thank you, Matthaya. That means a lot to me."

"I know."

17

KATHERA

"GOOD EVENING, Kieran," I said, tipping my head to him as I entered the shop.

"Hey." He lifted a hand in a half-hearted wave.

In an effort to keep myself busy and my mind occupied, I had asked Kieran to book a few extra appointments for the week.

"Uh, hey, I got a question," he said, putting down his phone and lifting a sticky note from the desk.

"Yes?" I popped behind the reception desk with him.

"Some guy called and wanted to know if you consider apprenticeships. I said I didn't think so, but he asked me to check with you anyway. Said he could forward you his portfolio if that would help.”

“I don’t,” I replied, shaking my head. “You said the right thing. I’m not interested in hiring any other tattoo artists right now.”

“Oh, he didn’t mean tattoos.”

“He didn’t?”

“He’s working on graphic novels. Says he’s been heavily inspired by your art and wanted to know if you’d consider critiquing or redlining his work, or mentoring him via email. He’s also interested in getting a tattoo from you.”

Since I was trying to keep things low-key, I really didn’t want anyone else hanging around the place. Having Kieran there was enough of a liability.

Derek had given me a chance and I’d have gone nowhere without that opportunity.

But I didn’t have time to teach someone.

“Tell him I’m not accepting apprenticeships right now, and apologize on my behalf.”

Kieran seemed disappointed with my answer, but then he shrugged and nodded. “Got it. You’re the boss.” He turned to his computer and started typing an email.

“As for the tattoo. Please ask him to send me more details on design, size, location—the usual. We can set up a consultation if it seems like a good fit.”

"Will do." Kieran saluted with two fingers and his eyes didn't leave the computer screen.

Kieran was usually quiet, something I liked about him. I didn't know if it was his nature, or if he was intimidated by me for any number of reasons. He had a good head on his shoulders, though, and there was an air about him that Matthaya and I agreed made him trustworthy.

I think he'd perked up at the thought of having an apprentice around the shop because he wanted someone else to talk to. Part-time work with only one artist did make the place eerily quiet, at times.

But that was the way I liked it.

I headed to my studio to prepare my equipment and look over my schedule of appointments. Kieran had texted me a list of some clients coming in for consultations, as well as another two who had already pre-paid for work.

I opened the autoclave and removed blue-tinted pouches from the metal trays inside. A quick go-over confirmed they had been properly disinfected—the plastic pouches had changed color from blue to clear, and indicator strips on the sides of each had changed from white to dark blue.

I set everything to the side on a safe, sterilized area of my workstation, and glanced at my ink cabinet.

As if he'd somehow known what I was thinking, Kieran poked his head around the corner and said, "I already placed orders for black and red. Should be in tomorrow, they told me. Blue looks good and we have plenty of white and everything else."

I grinned at him. "You're fantastic," I said. "Thank you for being one step ahead."

"I wanna keep my job," he replied with a smirk. "And you're welcome."

He swiveled around in his chair and moved back to the computer.

Two consultations and a mini skull tattoo later, I had begun work on a flash tribal dragon for a male client.

Derek had designed many of the flash tattoos in the shop. Over the years, I had contributed several, too—mostly macabre creatures mixed in with goddess-like figures with antlers and/or wings—complex original pieces popular with collectors. It had been months since I'd inked one of Derek's designs, but I decided I had to let go of the past and move on. This was a start.

Restless Ink was originally his, but when he renamed it for my art, it became a joint effort and he encouraged me to offer his flash sheets, too, to continue sharpening my skills on tribals.

I started on the dragon's wings, carefully tracing smooth strokes to the sides to flesh out the shapes of the wings, and then moving down to outline the main torso, back legs, and then tail. My canvas was remarkably quiet, though I couldn't complain; I was more efficient when my head was down and they didn't want to talk. I wasn't good at small talk anymore.

I changed out the needles and began filling in the design, beginning with the head. The buzzing of the machine drowned out my thoughts, white noise to my refined vampire hearing. A type of meditation, even, the repetitive sounds soothing the restless creature hidden beneath a human façade.

The sound of footsteps across the waiting room drew my face up. A silhouette of a tall figure blurred past the threshold of my studio, a glimpse of red and black colors.

"Kieran?" I raised my voice so he could hear me.

"Yeah, boss?" He rolled his chair into view. "What's up?"

"Who's that?" I nodded toward the lobby.

Kieran narrowed his eyes. "Uh. What?" He looked toward the waiting room and then back at me. "Who's who?"

I swear I...

"Give me just a minute, please," I spoke to my canvas,

and then stood and crept toward the doorway.

There was no one else in the waiting room.

"I was only on my phone for, like, a minute," Kieran said anxiously. "I don't think I missed anyone."

A brief sniff of the air confirmed no one else had entered.

"It's fine," I replied. "I must have been imagining things."

"Okay." Kieran shrugged.

I returned to my studio and took a seat.

"I apologize for that. I thought I saw someone."

My canvas just grinned in acknowledgment.

I lifted the tattoo machine and dipped the needles into fresh black ink. Slowly, I colored the curve of the wings, careful to keep the pressure even and strokes smooth so that it would heal cleanly.

Nearly finished, I swiveled around to dip my needles once more.

As I turned and lowered the machine toward the cup of black ink, a drop of bright crimson hit the tabletop.

"What?" I drew back the machine and lifted my hand away, looking around quickly to see from where the ink had spilled. I didn't leave open bottles sitting out.

There were no other colors in sight.

"Something wrong?" my canvas asked, leaning forward in his chair.

"No. Sorry." I shook my head and reached for a paper towel so I could wipe up the splash. If any had gotten into the black, it could have been contaminated.

I tossed the cup of black into the trash bin. Then I sprayed disinfectant on the area and wiped it down again, for good measure.

"Just a minute. Sorry for the delay. I need to get more ink for this last part. I... must have miscalculated."

He nodded in understanding.

I poured a new cup of black and reached for the tattoo machine.

That's when another drop of red hit the table. I pulled back and gritted my teeth.

Where was it coming from?

My hand twinged and I turned to set the tattoo machine down.

A bright red line dashed across the inside of my wrist and I jolted, releasing the machine so it hit the table with a thud. My client let out a grunt of pain as I inadvertently slammed my chair into his leg when I pushed back.

"I'm sorry!" I slid my chair away from him, hitting the wall behind me next.

My skin felt damp. I turned both wrists over—matching deep gashes split the skin and lines of red drizzled down my arms.

The overhead lights began to flicker and then the

room went black.

A flash of amber color drew my attention to the far corner of the ceiling. There was no mistaking Ve'tani's vivid eyes aglow with supernatural light. I bolted out of my chair just as the room lights flashed on again and she pounced, slamming me against the wall, shattering drywall. Her thin, but strong, fingers seized my arms and her nails pierced my flesh.

"This is your fault!" she rumbled, then lifted me off my toes and flung me against the studio floor, making the tiles crack beneath my weight.

As I scrambled to get up, she charged again. Her weight smashed into me, sending a crack up my spine, which paralyzed me on the cold floor. Claws tore across my wrists, deepening the wounds and lacerating tendons, until bone shimmered through pooling crimson.

"Why?" I opened my mouth to speak, but the word came out only as a whisper.

"Kathera!?" Derek's voice sounded from the lobby.

Derek! His name wouldn't form on my lips, but I tried.

He approached the threshold of the studio and stood in the archway, looking more human than ever.

Horror twisted his expression and his eyes went wide. "What the hell—"

Ve'tani roared and turned to face him, her thick velvet robe dragging through my blood.

Get out of here, Derek!

I bore down and used every shred of will to bring myself to my knees, slipping on the blood as I tried to come to my feet.

"Derek!" I screamed at him and reached out, my wrists limp. "Get away!"

Ve'tani, standing now, bolted toward him, wrapping her hands around his throat and lifting him up from the floor as if he were a doll. She tossed him across the room and a thunderous crash resonated through the walls.

His weak voice called for help.

Sirens blared outside. An ambulance horn sounded in the streets.

"Kathera!" An unintelligible voice spoke.

I looked around the room, but saw nothing but red.

So much blood.

"Kathera!"

The voice, again.

Then the sirens drew closer.

I dragged myself toward the lobby.

There was a young, dark-haired man standing there. He reached toward me and my mind raced, trying to put a name to the face.

I knew him. He smelled and looked familiar.

"K-Kieran?"

He came into focus and the room shifted shades, the

red fading.

"Are you okay?" he asked, panicky. "I didn't know what to do, so I called 911."

"You... what?" I gazed up at him. The shop lights had stopped flickering and the blood stains had disappeared.

Loud brakes hissed outside the shop. A large vehicle—an ambulance, or a fire truck. I couldn't tell.

The weakness dissipated and successfully I came to my feet. Everything in the waiting room and studio looked clean and there was no evidence of a violent confrontation.

My poor client stood in the corner of the room, terrified.

I looked at my wrists. Both gashes had vanished, too.

I shook my head with frustration. "But... Derek? Did you see him?" I glared at Kieran, who shook his head adamantly.

The shop door opened and two paramedics barged inside.

"No. No paramedics! What have you done?" I snarled at Kieran and he yelped and backed away.

"I'm sorry!" I shouted at him, struggling to repress the vampire rage building inside me.

The paramedics approached and asked how I was feeling.

"I'm fine. Please, leave me alone."

"Are you sure?" one of them asked. "You don't look well."

"She's always been really pale," Kieran chimed in, his voice shaking.

The frightened patter of his heartbeat reverberated in my brain.

"Please go. It was a false alarm," I said. "It was... just a panic attack. I'm fine. I just need rest."

The second paramedic looked over at Kieran and then back at me. "All right," he said. "I'll just need you to fill out this form, please, before we leave."

He pulled a clipboard out of his neon-yellow pack and handed it to me. "Just name and phone number will be enough."

I lifted a hand to take the pen from him, but I couldn't stop shaking.

"I'll take care of it." Kieran stepped up and took the pen. "I'm her receptionist."

"As long as someone fills it out," the paramedic replied flippantly.

I made my way over to a couch in the lobby and slowly lowered my weight onto it.

The flashing lights just outside the storefront made lines of red and white across the walls. I closed my eyes and lowered my head to try to calm down.

I heard Kieran thank the paramedics for coming so

quickly, and then the front door opened and closed twice. His heartbeat was finally returning to normal.

I'd completely forgotten about the client I'd been working on, until I overheard Kieran asking him to re-schedule. There was a little back and forth about costs and other specifics and then they stopped talking.

The door opened and closed again. Then I heard it lock.

Quiet footsteps grew near and the cushion flexed as weight sunk in beside me.

"I'm sorry about all that," Kieran said softly. "I didn't know what to do. You were freaking out in the studio and talking about blood. I-I—"

"Thank you for worrying about me." I opened my eyes and glanced over at him. There was genuine concern on his face and fear in his enlarged pupils.

"Is there *anything* I can do to help? Anything at all?"

I thought on it for a moment.

"Yes."

He perked up.

"Would you mind cleaning up for me tonight so I can head home early?"

"Sure. No problem at all. I just turned our sign off and I was gonna suggest you maybe go home and rest anyway. Do you need me to call your husband for you?"

"I'll be fine, but thanks."

I stood up from the couch and Kieran stood with me.

He wasted no time at all and immediately went into my studio to start cleaning up my table.

I wanted to go home, but I also didn't need Matthaya asking me why I was so on edge.

What the hell were all of those horrible visions? Why did I see Ve'tani trying to kill me again? That blood spilling out of my wrists... it felt so real.

And I saw Derek get attacked by her. Just like before. Only I'm sure I heard him calling for help, but I was stuck there on the floor, bleeding out.

Damn it. I didn't need this.

Matthaya was right. The decisions I made were right at the time. I couldn't let guilt destroy me.

I shouldn't let Derek destroy me...

I *needed* to purge myself of his presence.

Looking over at the framed images of his flash designs around the room, I contemplated tearing them down. But those designs were my lifeblood, too, and they made me who I am today. His designs shaped my career. It wasn't right of me to destroy such artwork. It wasn't the art's fault that I had burdens to bear.

But there was one thing I could let go of.

One thing I *should* have let go of long ago.

I walked into my studio and Kieran kept on like I

wasn't even there; he had a pair of earbuds in with rock music booming through them. He acknowledged me as I approached my workbench and stepped out of the way.

I withdrew a key from my pocket and used it to open the lock on the top drawer. It slid open and I reached inside for a small black box.

Then I closed the drawer and tapped Kieran on the shoulder. He looked at me and I mouthed the words, "I'm leaving now."

He smiled and nodded, and then I left the shop.

I passed the velvet jewelry box between my hands as I walked, deliberating if it was the right thing to do—the right way to let it go.

It was the only way.

I scaled the cemetery gate and landed with a thud on the other side. The sun had set and hazy moonlight illuminated my surroundings. I followed a long stone walkway, pausing to acknowledge my mother's grave before turning down a pathway to an area of the cemetery I had rarely ventured into.

There were fresh flowers on the memorial stone— likely from his mother—and a strange sensation came over me as I read the carved writing.

"Derek Michael Ashcroft. An Artist is Never Forgotten."

Reading it out loud was uncanny, because, in truth, no body lay below that stone.

There had been so much blood at the scene of the attack, that he had eventually been pronounced dead, his body never recovered.

I crouched down and swept away dead leaves that had gathered at the headstone. Maybe it wasn't an empty grave after all. There lay a man I had admired and cared about, a man who taught me all I knew about the craft I practiced today.

There lay a man who loved me, even when I couldn't return the sentiment.

I reached into my pocket and withdrew the black velvet box. I stared at it for a moment, judging whether to open it or leave it closed, settling on the latter.

"A 'yes' would have been a lie," I whispered, as I yanked a small patch of grass up and buried my nails into the ground to pull out a large handful of dirt. "I wouldn't lie to you, Derek." The box disappeared into the hole and I used both hands to cover it with fresh earth and resituate the tuft of grass on top with gentle pressure.

I had finally lain to rest some of my past, and that was the first step in coming to terms with it.

The wind blew, kicking up leaves around me and making bare trees waver and creak. I came to standing and brushed my hair back as it snaked wildly around my face.

As I turned to leave, the ground rumbled beneath my feet and I looked down. An explosion of dirt blinded me and I stumbled forward, nearly losing my balance.

I took another step, trying to shake the debris from my eyes, but I couldn't move; something tangled around my ankle. Through blurred vision, I saw what appeared to be a hand protruding from the grave, clutching me with frigid, bony fingers.

Dirt spilled onto the grass as a hideous, blue-white arm emerged. Then a head breached the surface of the earth, followed by shoulders and its other arm.

"*You* did this to me," it gurgled, straining to pull itself from the ground. The face tilted toward me, but I couldn't recognize it with its discolored bruising and blotchy, sagging skin.

I blinked several times and my vision cleared, just as the entity grasped my leg even harder, using me as leverage. Shredded skin dangled on the bones, but there was just enough left on its bare upper arm for me to recognize fragments of a distinct tattoo.

The corpse—Derek—glared up at me with dead eyes, his torso finally emerged. His chest had been torn open and his ribs exposed. Patches of flesh and fabric clung to his body and some vertebrae peeked out from behind the ribcage.

I took a step, but he grabbed my other ankle and I fell.

"I didn't do this to you!" My fingers pushed into damp earth as I scrambled backward, my heels wedging into the mud. "Ve'tani did this to you! She's the monster!"

The rotting corpse of what was left of Derek growled. "There's only one monster here." His skeletal fingers let go and he launched toward me. I screamed and covered my face, closing my eyes unintentionally.

A loud crack rang out and a tremor shook the earth. I opened my eyes and looked around. The corpse was gone, but as my gaze drifted up, I saw a deep fracture marring Derek's granite headstone.

I heard footsteps nearby.

18

KATHERA

"YOU CAN fix this, you know," Derek spoke, approaching slowly while offering an open hand to me. He was real and intact, aside from being a vampire. The decomposing body must have been a hallucination.

"Please, stop," I said, refusing to look at him.

"You used to feel safe with me," he said, bending down to take my hand and pull me to my feet. "Right?"

Saying no to him now was a lie, but after everything he'd done to me, I couldn't feel safe around him anymore. I bit my tongue and tried to hide my thoughts.

"I'm sorry I scared you earlier, but I needed to remind

you of what happened—why we're here now."

He stroked his fingers across my forearm and grasped my left hand. "All I needed from you was one little word. That's all it would have taken to make me happy. To make *us* happy." I felt pressure on my finger and glanced down to see a shimmering diamond solitaire ring covering my tattoo.

"Why would you throw away something so precious?" he continued. "You know I'd do anything for you."

"Then stop this!" I tried to jerk away from him again but couldn't. "You're not making me happy doing any of this. You're making my life hell. This is torture, and you know it. Please, stop punishing me for something I didn't do on purpose."

"Oh, but you did." He caressed my wrist. "You brought Matthaya and Ve'tani straight to my doorstep."

"I'm sorry she attacked you, but I didn't mean for it to happen."

"It's okay," he said. "You can make this right. I'll forgive you, if you make the correct choice this time."

He squeezed my hand. The diamond glittered beneath the moonlight.

"Well?"

How can I escape this?

"It's just one word," he whispered.

One word? He wanted me to say yes to his proposal—to accept it against my will even though I had already married another man. It didn't make sense to me, but somehow it made sense to him, and I was trapped in his twisted reality.

Maybe if Derek heard what he wanted, he'd stop tormenting me long enough to listen. Long enough to understand the truth about how I had felt about Matthaya from the beginning and how our fates were intertwined.

I had to do it, I thought.

I had to say...

"Yes."

There was a moment of complete quiet. The entire universe came to a standstill and the utter silence was unnerving.

I waited for Derek to speak again.

His hand came up and covered my eyes, making the cemetery go black.

"You'll be safe here," he said softly, all malice gone from his voice.

He removed his hand to reveal a warm, subtly lit bedroom with a large bay window and breathtaking view of the ocean. A massive white moon hung in the sky, shining like a beacon and glittering off waves rolling toward the shore. He prompted me to turn toward the other side of the room, where ruby-red candles perched in sconces and atop furniture lit the walls with a comforting yellow glow.

I could not pretend to ignore the grand bed in the middle of the room. Large, elegantly carved bedposts spiraled toward the ceiling. The crisp, fine linens were red as a rose, and decorations along the walls flowed in shades of autumn golds and browns.

Fears bubbled inside me, but the place exuded tranquility, and it was difficult to remain on edge with its warmth swallowing me up.

"I promise not to hurt you," Derek said in a calm, *human* tone. It was an eerie change of pace.

When he pressed a hand to the side of my arm and slid it down to meet my fingers and take my hand into his own, his skin felt warm and his grasp gentle—gentler than it had been since he'd been changed.

Derek came around to face me and reached up to fork his fingers through my hair, combing them behind my ear and resting his palm at the base of my neck. His other hand rose toward my collarbone, and he pressed it against my skin, near my heart.

"Your heart is racing," he said. "You don't have to be afraid anymore."

Since I'd been taken by the vampire disease, I'd had no pulse...

But sure enough, I felt something beating—thumping

against my ribcage. A patter of anxiety and anticipation fluttered in me, even as I knew it was wrong to feel.

I felt blood coursing through my veins and butterflies twirling in my stomach. All the overwhelming sensations washing over me were reminiscent of before—of the time when—

Derek's hand lifted from near my heart and came down to clasp me at my waist, his other hand shifting to my chin.

My heart raced and a breath caught in my throat as he lifted my face toward his and moved in to kiss me.

I thought to lift my arms and push him away.

I thought to shove him back.

And I could have... I think my body would have listened.

But despite all the rejection and disgust swelling inside, regardless of how much anger I'd felt for all he had done to me... a fog of conflicting feelings made me hazy and unafraid.

The anxious, very human flutter of my heart reminded me of how I had felt once before. Although I had not necessarily missed the sensation or regretted losing it, I did feel a sense of nostalgia and contentment as it consumed me again.

Or perhaps, Derek was loosening his grasp on my consciousness, now that I had stopped resisting.

He released me for a moment and then took me by the hand, walking me toward the crimson bed. I sat on the edge and my weight gently sunk into the softness. Derek joined me, his skin tone and body temperature warmer than before and unlike any vampire's.

Human.

There was a warm sensation on the back of my neck as his fingers brushed my hair away and he kissed my shoulder. My head tilted to the side.

In those shadows, alive with dancing candlelight and warm colors, my memories drifted away. I had forgotten who I was and who I had become. I had forgotten the malicious things Derek had done to me before, and the pain he had caused.

Our eyes met. He cupped my face in his hands and then he kissed my lips.

His warm touch put me at ease. I recalled what it had felt like to be loved by him, and what those feelings had once made me imagine, even yearn for, in secret. And for a fleeting moment, I thought I could remember someone else... but that memory evaporated and only *he* remained.

ജ ൫

A dull chime jarred me awake.

I opened my eyes to grass and dirt—the cemetery.

I pushed up onto my knees and glanced around. Derek's headstone loomed over me, the thick fracture no longer visible, but the small mound of dirt where I'd buried the ring was still fresh.

My phone chimed again.

I retrieved it from my pocket.

Matthaya had texted me several times over the last few minutes, asking for my whereabouts. It must have been exceedingly difficult for him to resist simply reaching out to me in my mind, but then... he *had* promised to give me privacy and space.

Did this mean he was unaware of everything that had happened in the vision with Derek?

Maybe it was better that way.

I scrambled to my feet and quickly typed a reply; I apologized for spending too long at my mother's grave.

He noted that I hadn't returned by my usual time.

I defended that the recent stressors had made me lose track of the hour.

He seemed to understand.

19

MATTHAYA

IT WASN'T like Kathera to ignore texts or to stay at the shop past scheduled hours. I was tempted to peek into her mind, but that ability was an unfortunate habit I had been trying to break.

I would not be Ve'tani.

I would not pry into my wife's thoughts or attempt to manipulate her actions.

With our marriage vows, we had made a promise to trust each other, and I would keep that promise, even as she struggled with her past. I trusted she would ask for help.

I felt Kathera approaching and went to the door to greet her before she could reach for the knob.

"I'm sorry if I worried you," she said, stepping up onto the porch.

"You didn't worry me. My habit of checking up on you has been difficult to break, but I am trying my hardest."

"I appreciate your trying."

I glanced over her quickly and couldn't ignore the patches of dirt discoloring her shirt and jeans.

"Where did all that come from?" I gestured toward her as she passed the threshold and entered. I closed the door behind her.

She froze momentarily, and I sensed a fleeting spark of discomfort flash through her.

"I sat at Mother's grave tonight," she replied. "Things have been tough lately, as you know."

I nodded.

"I know this sounds weird, but I had an urge to sit on the ground and just feel the earth beneath me, to be a little closer, I guess."

There was anxiety in her blood, but she successfully masked it in her voice. Something was off. I knew that her mother's gravesite, especially during this season, had been well maintained and was surrounded by a lush bed of grass. Even if there was exposed dirt or mud, she'd have to have taken quite a fall to get so much on her clothes.

Vampires were agile and sharp and we didn't experience human mishaps.

However, if Kathera had a reason to hide information from me, I would not prod her for it.

It was tempting to do so, but I *had* to let it go.

"I understand," I replied. "No need to explain."

"Thank you," she said with a small smile. "I will try to be more conscious of your feelings if I decide to do something like that again."

The shadows under her eyes had darkened and there was a hint of hunger brewing in her.

"Do you need something?" I asked. She looked very tired. Fine lines of red forking veins were visible on the skin around the corners of her eyes, an indicator of stress.

"If you don't mind," she replied. "Thank you."

I went into the basement to retrieve a bottle of blood.

As I returned up the steps, she asked, "Did you get in touch with the doctor?"

"Yes," I replied, entering the kitchen. I opened the cupboard and removed a pair of wine glasses. "I have sent her the additional information she requested." The glasses clinked against the marble countertop. "She's making plans to visit at the end of the month, while the campus is on holiday."

"That soon?" Kathera seemed surprised by my

efficiency.

I pushed a metal corkscrew into the bottle and turned it. "Will it be a problem?" I pulled back on the cork and removed it.

"No. I was under the impression that she required more details before finalizing her plans."

"As I had mentioned earlier," I continued, filling her glass halfway with blood, "I have worked in antiquities dealings before." I poured a glass for myself and then replaced the cork. "I was able to provide her with enough detail to authenticate the pieces without her being here, but she would still like to see them, and discuss her findings with us personally."

I had also offered to pay her stay for a few extra days, so that she might take in the local sights. I thought her company and intellect may put my wife's mind at rest, and it was worth the small fortune to get the doctor to take the trip if only for that reason. "The opportunity will also allow us to ask additional questions."

"You're right," Kathera said with a subtle nod. I passed her a glass of blood. "Thank you for discussing that with her. I look forward to meeting her in person." She took a sip from the glass and paused to savor it.

"You appear quite tired," I said quietly and then sipped from my glass. "Did everything go all right tonight?"

She tipped her glass back and drank from it again

before answering.

"Yes."

"And Kieran? Is he still working out?"

"Yes. Kieran is a great help. I'm grateful you suggested we hire him."

I wanted to ask her about Derek, but there was so much tension in the room. Over what, I could not tell.

She finished her drink and set the glass on the counter with a subtle clink. Her wrist was exposed to me briefly and I noted that the bite wound was barely visible.

I finished the last of my blood and then set the glass down beside hers.

"Your wrist looks better," I said.

She cupped it in her other hand and held it close to her chest. "Yes. It does."

I tried very hard to bite my tongue.

"I'm fine," she said before I could ask. "I would let you know if anything had changed."

"Thank you," I replied.

I appreciated the sentiment, but she was not telling the truth...

KATHERA

ONLY A few days had passed before Derek visited me in my sleep again. It was different this time. I had stopped resisting his advances and he had stopped torturing me with horrific acts and visions.

Derek had the power to infiltrate my mind any time he pleased—made obvious by his interjection at the cemetery—but now that I had given in to his demands, he left my sanity intact while I was awake.

Guilt drained me of what few emotions I had left; I was a fool for surrendering—for not fighting back or telling my husband the truth.

But how could I?

Telling Matthaya meant a death sentence for Derek. A physical altercation could also put Matthaya's well-being at risk.

They were only dreams, but they felt like reality.

Derek swept me up into his intimate fantasy each time I slumbered.

I would wake with fractured memories of the events and a wretched feeling of self-loathing.

It was stupid of me to play along. I was only pretending to consent to it all, but that consent enveloped and manipulated me like a drug. I couldn't escape it.

When I stopped fighting, Derek stopped exhibiting abusive behavior, forcing my actions, and questioning my faithfulness. It was... *easier* this way.

I'd given in to his desires, and I felt nothing but remorse.

I enjoyed none of it, and when I awoke, confusion riddled my thoughts.

The cycle continued.

During those moments, I was forced to forget my real husband.

21
MATTHAYA

KATHERA SLEPT beside me, her eyes closed tightly, her body still as stone, and an unusual calm placating her.

On the outside...

Subtle distress radiated from her mind. She'd been trying to hide it from me for a while, but I'd witnessed her wake disoriented several times and then brush it off once she'd gotten her bearings. Intense hunger could cause some disruptions, but her symptoms were too close together and persisted even after she'd consumed blood.

I could not disregard the incidents anymore.

I had to learn the truth, even if it meant going against my word and prying into her mind. There was nothing I wanted more than to assure her safety, but I could not do that if she continued to keep secrets.

It was ironic that following my confrontation with Ve'tani, and shortly after our agreement to ignore Derek, he had begun to leave her alone.

Derek was not one to back down.

"I'm sorry I have to do this," I whispered, brushing a lock of hair from her face.

I closed my eyes and lay down beside her, willing the makeshift barrier between our minds to collapse so that I could slide into her subconscious again. It had been a long time since I had attempted such a strong connection, yet there was no resistance whatsoever.

I was transported to an imaginary place inside her mind, where heavy fog swallowed me up and the air embraced me with cold arms. I took a step, my shoe crunching on twigs. A gust of breeze blew and the fog began to separate, revealing a pathway lined with dead, skeletal trees along an old dirt road. A frigid wet kiss hit my cheek; I shook my head and swiped away the lone snowflake.

A flurry began drifting down from a cloudy gray sky, and when I exhaled, a puff of white came from my lips.

Was this one of Kathera's dreams? It was vivid and clear. She had told me several times that she had never seen snow but wished that she could. Maybe this was a place of inspiration for her.

I rubbed my arms and shivered. It was so very cold, though.

Snow accumulated quickly and I continued walking, my shoes vanishing beneath white between steps. I followed what I perceived was a pathway through the trees, shuddering as the freezing air licked the back of my neck, sending a chill up my spine. I popped my jacket collar up and pulled the flaps of my coat closed.

Large tufts of cottony snow blew past, reducing visibility.

The place started looking less and less like a creative haven and more like—

I heard the unmistakable sound of a girl crying.

"Kathera?"

Cold air nipped at my cheeks and I lowered my face to shield it with my collar. That's when my gaze fell upon a trail of small footprints dotting the snow. I followed them, clutching tightly to my coat as the frigid breeze battered me and made my fingers tingle. The footprints led me to a massive old tree, where they winded around to the other side and brought me face to face with a small, slender figure sobbing on the ground.

Her knees were to her chest and her face was against them. She wore a dingy, tattered white dress with bare feet poking out from beneath the shredded lace hem, highlighted with the beginning shades of frostbite. Her faded brassy-red hair was flecked with large snowflakes and the curls appeared frozen against the back of her dress as she heaved distressed breaths.

A squeezing, nauseating heaviness pooled in my stomach as I bent to touch her on the shoulder. She gasped and looked up at me fearfully.

There was no mistaking her face—those pale blue eyes.

Centuries after her death, a perfect image of a sixteen-year-old Kathryn moved and breathed before me, trapped in some remote place in Kathera's memory.

But she had changed.

Her smooth, youthful complexion had lost much of its color and the corpse-like tones of her flesh were reminiscent of my own unflattering condition. Pale, gray-blue undertones emphasized the deep inset curves of her malnourished body and face, and darkened veins were faintly visible through her thin, fragile skin.

"Matthaya?" she spoke through papery lips, in the Irish accented voice I had not heard in several hundred years.

The roundness of her cheeks had sunken into sharp curves of flesh clinging to bone. She reached out to me with a frail hand and a grave look of sadness welling in her eyes.

"I am sorry, Matthaya," she uttered, her hand shaking as she strained to reach for me with emaciated arms discolored by old, yellowing bruises. I came down beside her on the ground and swiftly took her hand into mine. It was cold as ice and ghostly in comparison to my own.

"I-I tried to stop him," she muttered through a stream of tears. "I was not strong enough, but I tried."

"I am here now," I whispered calmly, and then reached my other hand up around to the back of her head to grasp her gently and pull her close to my chest.

She plummeted against me and her heartbeat quickened as she trembled, her tears nearly freezing against my shirt as I embraced her. Each quivering inhalation sent a ripple of pain through my own body that I had not felt in ages. There was a squeezing sensation in my chest, and it was as if my heart hurt just to hold her.

"Tell me what happened," I spoke softly.

She coughed on congestion and tears and then sat up just enough to wipe her face with her thin, child-like hands. The sickness inside me intensified as I took in her wretched condition.

"Can you still love me?" she asked, heaving short, sharp breaths.

I lifted a hand to her face and cupped her delicate,

ashen cheek in my palm. "What do you mean by that?" I asked.

Kathryn overlaid her fingers on mine and pressed against me as she closed her eyes. "Can you still love me now that..." she shuddered again and looked me in the eye, "another man has ruined me?"

With cold air pounding against me and my heart throbbing with distress, it took me a moment to understand what she had said. I had been Kathryn's first love, and she mine.

She couldn't have meant someone from our time.

No.

She *must* have meant Derek.

"Did he touch you?" I clenched my teeth and the words came out as a growl.

She whimpered and shrank away from me.

"I am sorry," I said, trying to calm her. "I did not mean to frighten you."

She gazed up at me, worried.

And then I remembered her question and promptly answered, "Yes. Yes, I can and will love you still."

A small smile curled across her lips and she lifted her hands to her heart. "I tried to resist him, but I could not. Please, understand that I tried."

"You do not have to cry anymore," I whispered, trying to reassure her. "I am here, and I love you, regardless."

I embraced her tightly again and then propped my back up against the trunk of the tree so she could rest against me.

"I wanted it to be you," she said weakly against my chest. "I was certain it was to be you."

"Shh." I hugged her and brushed a hand over her stiff, frozen copper curls. Snowflakes settled on my skin and my jaw tightened from the aching cold.

Her body continued to pulse against me as she cried, but she slowly began to calm. Her fingers came up toward my collar, where they grasped onto and wrinkled my shirt, just as she had done many years ago. There was a part of me that took pleasure in being able to feel her there again.

And a part of me that hated it.

Kathryn possessed a ghostly, frail form I had never seen before, and the fragility of her condition sickened me. The thought of what Derek must have done to have forced Kathera to such a breaking point, made me burn with rage.

I hid my feelings and thoughts from Kathryn, so as to not terrify the poor, tortured thing, but they billowed fervently within me.

I would not let *him* live...

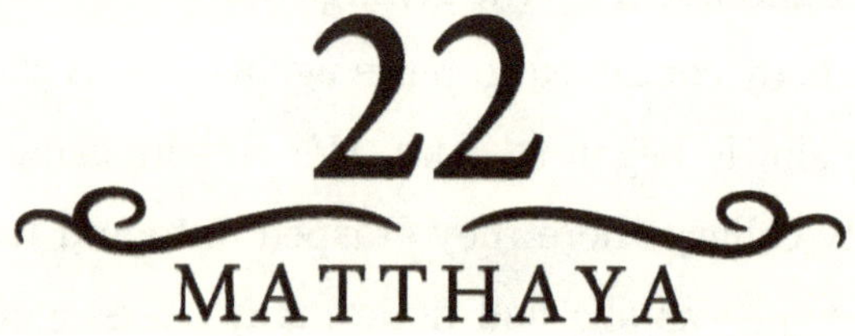

22

MATTHAYA

THERE WAS no telling when Derek would take control of Kathera's mind again, but I was not about to abandon Kathryn. She clung to me, though our closeness could not fight back the chill, and she continued to tremble until her teeth chattered.

"My love." I brought a hand toward her face to gently coax her to look at me. "You are so very cold. Please, let me help you."

I stood slowly, carefully moving so as to not touch any of her bruises, and then removed my long coat.

"Y-you will f-freeze," she uttered.

"I will be fine." I knelt in the snow and helped her

slide her fragile, pale arms into sleeves that were far too long for her. She pulled the flaps closed tightly at her chest and tried to smile in thanks, but the biting cold forced a quivering frown to drag down her lips.

The cold consumed me, too, and uncomfortable, painful sensations I had not experienced in centuries continued to crash over me.

But I had to move forward and push through the discomfort for her.

It was Kathera's mind—fueled by splintered remains of Kathryn's soul—and the horrible manifestations there could not harm *me*.

The snow fell faster, flakes taking on large shapes which continued to pile up. I looked around, squinting to gaze past dead trees and blustering swirls of snow, into the distance. There was no shelter of any kind.

Then I looked down at Kathryn. She had slumped back against the tree and was hunched over with her feet pulled close to her chest again. Her toes were turning a ghastly shade of blue.

A gust of wind roared past, sweeping over me like the touch of Death—its icy kiss making me gasp and my teeth clatter. I had to get her out of the damn cold.

Without asking permission, I reached down and scooped Kathryn into my arms. She whimpered, briefly, but then threw her arms around my neck and shoulders and clasped onto me as best she could.

I trudged through the snow against the deadly wind that nipped my face. Kathryn clutched onto me with all her effort, though her grasp still felt very weak.

But the distance trekked revealed nothing but more emptiness and cold—a barren wasteland of frigid white.

"It is h-hopeless," she murmured. "We will perish here. Leave me for my sins. S-save yourself."

It was then that I realized Kathryn's subconscious was guiding us, and that it was her own brutal self-criticisms that must have been isolating us to the treacherous place. If she truly believed she had been trapped in eternal nothingness, then that is all we would see.

But, perhaps, if I could make her believe otherwise...

If I could make her think, for a moment, that we had found sanctuary from the cold, then—

"Kathryn, look," I said, raising my voice over the whistling wind. "I see shelter ahead. A small cabin, by the looks of it."

There was no cabin in the distance, only skeleton trees clattering in a foreboding ocean of white.

I raised a cold, painful hand and pointed up ahead.

"There, I see it," I said.

She turned her head slightly and squinted as she tried to see it, too.

I took a few more steps, lowering my head to brace

against the cold while holding Kathryn close against me.

"Perhaps..." she spoke.

I continued to slog through snow that was now calf-deep and felt a sudden lull in the air. The wind quieted down, and as I lifted my face to peer into the distance again, the heavy snow shower slowed to a gentle dusting.

"I see it now," Kathryn whispered.

I looked up ahead at what appeared to be a small cabin.

With the wind having died down and the snow coasting to sprinkling, visibility became better and it took only a few more steps before the building came into focus.

As my bones began to stop aching, and my hands regained some feeling, I picked up pace until we reached the front door of the structure. It wasn't in the best shape, but it would suffice for escape from the cold, assuming no one was inside.

"It looks abandoned," I said, in an effort to soothe Kathryn's distressing suspicions.

The truth was, I could not tell if it truly was empty or not, but I had to lie to make sure her fears did not conjure someone's presence.

I set her down a few feet from the door and asked her to stay put while I investigated.

The wood panels were old with some weather damage and cracking, but it appeared structurally sound on the outside. I crept up the makeshift steps leading to the door and pushed the metal handle. The door drifted open, allowing me to see inside—into the empty room.

I poked my head through the threshold.

There was a meager fireplace on one side of the room, and a few pieces of broken furniture. A dilapidated chair and table had been left behind, and a few old wool blankets were piled in the corner. The windows were frosted and dark, but a small amount of light managed to come through. The whole place was dusty and hadn't been touched in years.

I turned back toward Kathryn. "It looks safe," I said. "Come."

She scrambled up the steps and into the cabin, and I closed the door tightly behind her. A sudden gust of wind sent a flutter of snow through the broken window on the other side of the room. I made haste to scoop up a rag from the nearby blanket pile and seal the hole by forcing it into the crack in the glass.

A piercing sensation shot through my hand and I hissed. I withdrew my fingers from the window gap and a line of blood trailed down my hand.

"You cut yourself!?" Kathryn rushed toward me and took my hand into hers.

The wound stung, but it wasn't too deep.

She bent down, tore a piece of petticoat lace from beneath her dress, and then wrapped it around my hand. My blood stained the white with red, but then the bleeding ceased shortly after. I had not expected Kathryn to be so responsive to something of this nature.

"Thank you," I said, looking her in the eye. Some color was returning to her skin already.

She smiled weakly, but smiled, nonetheless.

"We should make a fire," I said, gesturing toward the fireplace. She nodded and looked over at the broken furniture.

"Will that burn?" she asked.

"It should." I crouched down to look up inside the fireplace flue, placing a hand near the opening. There was a subtle draft, indicating it wasn't clogged.

We searched the cabin for some kindling and managed to find an old pillow stuffed with straw. I combined it with broken furniture legs to start a scant fire which burned just long enough for me to gather more wood from outside. Some of it was damp from the snow, but there was a small pile near the cabin that had been graciously left by the previous occupants in a covered place.

I shook the dusty blankets out outside and then tossed them onto the floor in front of the fire. Kathryn sat down with her legs stretched out in front of her and her feet flexing in the flickering golden light.

"Thank you," she said, looking over at me as I came down to sit beside her. She was still wearing my coat, which draped her small, malnourished body like a cloak.

"You do not need to thank me," I replied.

"I would be dead without you," she said, gazing at me with a small, grateful grin curling her lips. She slipped my jacket down off her arms and laid it out near the fire to dry. Her eyes met mine again. The dark shadows under them were less apparent now, and the bruises marring her arms seemed lighter.

"How is your hand?" She slid a little closer to me.

I unraveled the lace and revealed the slit across my palm. "I will be okay," I replied, flexing my fingers. "It does not hurt anymore."

"Good."

A chill came over me and I shuddered.

"Matthaya?" Kathryn moved even closer. She looked me over quickly. "Your clothes are drenched with melted snow." She came to her feet and gathered up the blanket she had been sitting on. "Remove them, or else you will catch your death!"

It was strong and sickening—the chilling cold washing over my skin, making goose bumps rise up across my arms as I trembled involuntarily.

I tried to work my shirt buttons free, but I couldn't stop shaking. When I finally grasped onto one, squeezing my fingers together made the wound in my hand flex open and sent shooting pain through me.

I grunted and tried again.

"Here," Kathryn said, sitting up on her knees beside me and inching closer. She reached up and easily undid the buttons. Then she peeled the wet shirt down my shoulders and helped me pull it free of my arms.

She retrieved the nearby blanket and draped it over my back, rubbing my shoulders briskly to help warm me. Then she made herself comfortable on the floor again.

"Thank you," I said, shakily.

We sat before the dancing fire for several minutes—perhaps even half an hour—before one of us spoke again.

It was Kathryn who turned her face to me, opened her mouth, and said, "Did you mean what you said back there in the woods?"

The chill had finally left me and I felt much warmer under the heavy wool blanket. I pulled it up over my shoulders enough that I could free my hands from holding onto it and then reached over to her.

"Yes." I clasped my fingers around one of her hands. "I did."

"Does it not bother you?" She swallowed hard and clenched her jaw. Then she swept a hand down her skirt and took a deep breath.

"We were meant to be together," I said calmly. "Nothing will change how I feel about you."

"But I feel disgraced. Used. How will I ever free myself of these memories?"

"You may not be able to forget them," I said, "but we can create new memories—better ones—and leave no room for the others."

She looked up into my eyes and a sense of relief came over her. "You are very wise, Matthaya," she said. "More so than I will ever be."

I chuckled.

"Why do you laugh?" she asked, narrowing her eyes.

"I am nothing, and I come from nothing. Do not insult your intelligence by comparing yourself to me. You are brave and wise."

"Am I?" She tilted her head and glared. "Am I wise for finding myself here? For allowing that man to...?"

"That is not what I meant. You helped me when I cut my hand, and you assisted me with the fire. You were even smart enough to get me out of that wet shirt so that I could warm up with a blanket. You are far from foolish."

"This was my fault," she said.

"*None* of this was your fault. Do not blame yourself for *his* actions. His sins are not your own, and he will pay for his deeds."

Kathryn fell quiet and looked down at her hands.

"Maybe you are right," she whispered.

There was another long, uncomfortable bit of silence before she spoke again.

"But," she started, and then let out a brief chuckle beneath her breath. "But I am still a fool," she said, reaching to brush her warm fingers through my hair.

I felt a thumping in my chest—my pulse quickening. I had not felt my own heartbeat in ages.

"I am a fool who is hopelessly in love with you, and who wishes only for your love in return. A fool who would rather die than go on without you. All these thoughts and fears have brought me to this place of sorrow."

"Do not let doubt seize your mind ever again," I replied, ensnared by the glistening reflection of fire in her fair blue irises. "You will always have my love."

Kathryn stared at me. "Even now?" she asked, searching for the truth.

I nodded. "Even now."

My heart thundered in my chest as she threaded her fingers through my hair and then kissed me.

23
MATTHAYA

I AWOKE with a fleeting sensation of warmth fading from my fingertips.

Kathera lay beside me, and a vivid memory of the vision I had shared with Kathryn was swiftly escaping my mind, slipping away like water through cracked glass.

Everything had felt so real in her mind.

The frigid cold threatening me with frostbite and hypothermia.

The heat of the fire.

The warmth of her touch.

The pain of my wound.

I turned my hand—nothing but pristine skin where the cut once was.

But a distant memory of warmth on my lips remained. Kathryn's kiss...

I brushed the back of my hand across Kathera's cheek. Her skin was smooth and her expression made of such peace and beauty, unlike before, when distress tainted her blood.

Then I looked at the fireplace mantel, to the portrait of Kathryn sitting there. Only moments ago, I had seen her face in the flesh, her eyes alive with hope and passion, and her body warm when I embraced her.

The experience allowed clarity to permeate my mind, and I had an epiphany.

We needed to confront Derek.

A whispering voice reverberated through my mind, and I suddenly remembered.

Kathryn had told me where to find him...

঺ ঻

Kathera opened her eyes and looked at me, bewildered.

"What is it?" she asked, slowly sitting up.

"I need you to come with me," I said. The firm tone of my voice insinuated that there was no other option.

Still, she hesitated. "Where to?"

"We will settle this now."

Her eyes widened. "How do you know where he is?"

"You told me, in a dream."

Kathera gazed at me with a look of confusion on her face. She had not remembered any of the vision, it seemed. Kathryn's memories, and even her continued existence within her, had been lost to her subconscious.

"And what will you do once you find him?" she asked. "I've already begged you not to—"

"He needs to see the truth," I interrupted. "He needs to know who you really are."

"I'll go with you under one condition."

"Yes?"

"Promise me you won't take his life."

I narrowed my eyes at her. "His life was taken when Ve'tani changed him."

She sneered. "Promise me you won't... *end* him."

"I have a plan." I reached for her arm—the one with the bite mark on it—and turned it over so that I could see the faded black veins. "One that should put an end to *this* instead." I released her wrist and headed for the front door.

Under the cover of night, we set out to find Derek's feeding ground.

Just a few miles outside the city, an old apartment complex had been abandoned and condemned by the government. Yellow caution tape lay in shredded strips across piles of rotting refuse. The buildings had sunken unevenly into the unstable ground and crumbling brick walls looked as though they may collapse from even the slightest gust of wind.

The complex's dreadful, dangerous condition didn't stop squatters from taking up residence. Although evidence of their presence remained, I did not hear or see any humans in the area.

Kathryn was right to send me here. The scent of blood saturated the air, indicating this had been a place of slaughter.

Potholes punctured the barren street. Windows had been shattered and shards of glass left strewn across the ground. Shingles lay scattered across the walkways of fractured concrete. The numbers on the sides of the front doors were rusted and many of them missing. Paint peeled up from the doorframes and all the light fixtures had been broken, wiring exposed.

Life had existed here... once.

Now the strong scent of death and decay filled the air.

"Why would he be here?" Kathera asked.

"Because the people he found here had been forgotten.

They were easy targets."

I tried hard to recall exactly what Kathryn had told me in the vision. She had given me a place and a number—the building, I think.

17?

No.

217.

I remembered it clearly now—a number dangling from a cracked doorframe.

The door closest to us read "203." We kept moving.

"There," I said, pointing to the building with numbers just as Kathryn had described to me.

"Is this it?" Kathera asked.

I nodded and then held out a flattened hand, indicating that she should wait for me to investigate.

As I approached the door, I could see the lock was not engaged and that it had been left ajar. I peered through the opening and a wave of fresh blood smell wafted through, hitting me hard and triggering my vision to shift into predator mode. My surroundings took on subtle silhouettes of color, jagged lines of red and yellow.

I pushed open the door and took a step inside. There was blood along the doorframe. I looked down. Blood had been smeared across the tattered carpet and linoleum as if someone or something had been dragged through the building. By the smell of it, it was human, but more than one person's scent saturated the air.

I followed the trail to the back door. It opened up to a large grassy area—what appeared to have once been a dog park, but with the fences mostly collapsed and large patches of frayed chain-link gnarled up in coils along the perimeter.

I heard a quiet shuffle of feet.

Just as I sensed his aura, Derek dropped down from a rooftop. I ducked, narrowly avoiding him as he landed in front of me. I backed away a few steps and straightened up.

Kathera had just come out from around the other side of the building and was approaching us cautiously. I hadn't wanted her to get involved, but...

"What have you done here?" Kathera asked.

Derek snarled at her. "We have to survive, don't we?" he replied. "We can't all be like your perfect prince charming here. Maybe they don't taste great, but it's better than the putrid pig blood he feeds you."

"We drink that so we don't have to kill," she defended.

"And what's wrong with a little killing?" Light sparked through his eyes. "It's what we're made for. These people don't belong here. Hell, they don't belong anywhere." He bared his fangs and hissed at me. "How did you know where to find me, anyway? Did Ve'tani tell you?"

"I said nothing!" Ve'tani bellowed from above.

I veered my head and looked up. Ve'tani was perched on the rooftop next door, her bright amber eyes glistening.

"Then how did you find me?" Derek glared.

"I'm Kathera's Sire," I replied. "You're not the only one who can see into her mind."

"Lucky break," Derek said. "I must have been," he wiped his thumb across a bloodstain on his lower lip, "preoccupied." Kathera approached and stood beside me as we ventured into the field, to put some space between the three of us. Derek followed and Ve'tani remained on her perch atop the building, watching us intently.

Something told me I didn't have to worry about her, yet.

"You can't stop me," Derek continued. "You know what will happen if you interfere again." Then he grinned at Kathera. "And *you* know that I can take control whenever I want. Not that you've needed much coercing lately."

Kathera shook her head.

"Or did you not tell *him* about that?" Derek continued.

There was fear and a plea for help wavering through her consciousness.

Had she been hiding that from me all this time!?

It didn't matter anymore. What mattered was that this was going to stop.

Today.

"I'm here to help her," I said, glancing at her with a softened expression and a sincere, calm tone. "I'm here to help you *and* Kathryn."

Derek shot a glance at Kathera and then back at me. "Who?" he asked with a snarl.

Kathera's eyes rolled back and her knees buckled. I lunged and caught her in my arms before she hit the ground.

"I think it's time you learned the truth about who we are," I said.

"The truth?" Derek laughed angrily. "I know exactly what I am. You're the one who pretends to be something else."

"Not you," I replied. "Us." I embraced Kathera tightly.

I made a conscious effort to slip into her mind and, as I did, Derek took a step closer. My wings broke free, tearing open the back of my shirt, and then came up around us like a shield.

He froze in place and growled, his eyes igniting with a vivid red-orange glow; he knew better than to attack while my wings were out.

I concentrated again on accessing Kathera's mind, and this time I was successful.

My surroundings went dark, and although my body was awake in the real world, my consciousness had linked up with Kathera's, and time had stopped in the alternate dimension of her mind.

A faint flicker of light grew from the pitch black—sputtering lamps flashed on and off in the distance, dimly lighting a long hallway I'd seen once before.

A rustle of footsteps and the sound of a struggle came from down the hall. I squinted and gazed in the direction of the noise.

Derek manifested there, and he was holding Kathera tightly near his chest with her arms locked behind her back. Despite her angry grunts and her furious attempt to get away, she couldn't escape his grasp.

"You need to face the truth, yourself," Derek said. "You've lost control."

"That's one thing you have very wrong," I replied. "I don't control Kathera, nor do I control the way she feels about me. I don't need to, because we trust each other."

"Trust did *me* a lot of good." Derek scoffed. "I trusted her and she pined for you behind my back! And you... you got me turned into... *this*. I don't believe in trust anymore. I believe in taking what I want."

"Kathera is my wife," I said, "and you'll never have her love, or Kathryn's."

Kathera cried out and her body began to shrink, her frame becoming smaller, child-like, and her entire form changing into that of a young copper-red-haired girl in a white, tattered dress covered in dried blood stains.

Derek released her, thrusting her away with disgust. "Who the hell are you!?"

I gestured for Kathryn to come and she ran as fast as her small, bare feet could take her, barreling into me and clutching onto my jacket.

Derek bared his sharp teeth at her and snapped in her direction. She yelped and huddled closer to me.

"All this time," I spoke, "you were trying to take Kathera away from me, but you had no idea who she was on the inside. Look at what you've done. Look into the eyes of the girl you raped!"

Kathryn trembled beside me; I wrapped an arm around her to comfort her.

"I-I never touched that girl!" Derek said furiously. "Who the hell is she and what did you do with Kathera?" He looked at Kathryn and then back at me. "What did you do with her?"

"Show him what he did to you," I said to Kathryn. She whimpered and shook her head, shuddering with fear. "You must show him," I suggested again, stroking the back of her head. "Please."

She gazed up at me with frightened blue eyes.

"Be strong," I added with a confident smile. "I'm here."

She took a deep breath and nodded.

Derek glared suspiciously at her as she slipped from

my grasp and took slow steps toward him, straining to muster the courage to approach the enraged beast.

"*You* did this to me," she uttered, her voice breaking and barely audible, at first. She glanced back at me and I tipped my head reassuringly, giving her the strength to return her gaze to Derek. "All I wanted was to be with him," she continued, "and you took that away from me. You..." She stepped closer to him and stared up into his dark brown eyes. "You forced me to partake in terrible things—things I did not want to do."

"You're just some kid. I didn't do anything to you," Derek snarled. "I didn't—"

Kathryn lifted her arm up and turned it over so he could see the inside of her wrist. The skin was colored with black and blue veins where he had bitten her, and her upper arms were still marred with bruises.

"No! I wouldn't—" He began to panic, looking for a way out. I felt his hold on her consciousness weakening as he contemplated a way to escape.

Kathryn took one step closer, now within arm's reach of him. He growled, but she held her ground.

"I am willing to forgive you," she said. "If you free me." She lifted her fingers toward his face, but he jerked away and hissed.

The hall went pitch black.

KATHERA

I CAME to in an uncomfortable position on the ground, in Matthaya's arms, cloaked in the darkness of his wings cupped around us. After seeing that I had come to, his wings folded back behind him and he helped me to my feet.

Derek stood in the distance gazing at us with a look of disgust. I didn't know why he was staring at me like that, or what had happened just moments ago. All I could remember was approaching with Matthaya and then everything went black, and I awoke shielded by his wings.

I realized then why Matthaya had told me to wait out

front; the strong scent of blood in the air agitated me. I had to use all my restraint to stop my hunting instincts from triggering.

I took a step closer to Derek. The angry, feral energy that had radiated from him before did not seem as apparent, and I did not feel as threatened.

"Let me talk to him, please," I said, looking briefly at Matthaya.

He flinched with discomfort, and thought to stop me, but then lowered his head and nodded.

"Why are you doing this?" I asked Derek. "Why can't you let me go?"

"I don't understand," he replied as I approached. He looked over my shoulder, at Matthaya, and then back at me. "How did I screw up so badly? What the hell did I do to push you away? To make you... cheat?"

Is that what this was really about? He thought I had cheated on him?

There was nothing further from the truth.

"Do you know how hard it was when we lived together?" he continued. "Loving you with everything I was, while you kept secrets from me? I watched your nightmares bring you to tears in your sleep. And I had to listen to you calling out for *him* even as I lay beside you. You pushed me out of your heart and I was helpless to change your decision. I just want to know why. What did I do wrong?"

"I-I wasn't cheating on you," I said. "The truth is, there's more to this story than you know." I looked back at Matthaya briefly and then clasped my cross pendant between my thumb and index fingers before looking Derek in the eye again. "To *our* story.

"This cross belonged to the daughter of an English Baron in the 17th century. The very same Baron who had kept Matthaya as an indentured servant, and whose daughter would eventually grow to love a boy she was not allowed to be with."

A look of dread crept across Derek's face and he pushed it back with a growl.

"Matthaya was taken by Ve'tani and his death pushed the Baron's daughter to commit suicide. That girl's name was Kathryn. Part of her lives on in me, and with that part, a love for Matthaya."

Derek's jaw tightened and he grimaced. "That was her?"

I didn't understand what he had meant, but I continued. "When I was with you, the nightmares were memories of her suicide. I didn't understand them at the time, but they tormented me every night. I remembered everything. Drowning. Being swept under the waves while my limbs were entangled in kelp and debris. I remembered dying because I *was* Kathryn."

Derek looked toward the ground. "Damn," he uttered beneath his breath. Our eyes met again and intense sorrow tugged at his lips. He curled both hands into fists and shook his head angrily.

"I didn't know. I-I didn't understand," he said. "I—" He lifted a hand as if he might try to touch my face, but I felt Matthaya step closer, leading Derek to withdraw. "How could I have? I didn't know something like that was even possible." His gaze lowered, a flicker of yellow-orange light coiled through his eyes, and he shuddered. "All this time, I thought you'd betrayed me. That you'd—"

"I wouldn't have done that to you," I said. "I trusted you, and I didn't want to hurt you."

"So no matter what," he pointed at my left hand, "you would have said no?"

Our eyes met.

"Yes. I wanted to tell you sooner, but I didn't expect everything to happen like that. I was waiting for the right time to let go. It was just so hard. I didn't want to be alone, but I also felt that we weren't meant to be together. I'm sorry for the way I treated you. For misleading you. I didn't mean any of it. I was broken and stupid. And when Matthaya walked away, it devastated me."

"I believe you," Derek said quietly. His voice was softer than usual, with an air of defeat.

Matthaya approached us.

"We are not so unalike, you and I," he said to Derek.

"I doubt that." He refused to make eye contact with either of us.

"The foolish young love Kathryn and I harbored for each other brought us to our sorry fates." He took a step closer to Derek, who stiffened in defense. "But we were given a second chance. And, in a way, so were you. It is possible to move on. But you have to free her first."

Derek's shoulders slumped and he lowered his head in shame. "I-I don't know how."

"I am still here," a hoarse voice sounded from nearby; we all turned to look back at Ve'tani, who was glaring at us from atop the roof.

She leapt down, sending a flurry of shingles into the air, and landed with a thud nearby. She came to standing, brushed off her cloak, and shook her golden curls back over her shoulders.

"*I* may be able to help," she said, glaring at me and then at Matthaya. "Not that I should, but I have grown weary of this spectacle, and the constant banter coiling through my brain."

Derek perked up. "How? What do I do?"

She groaned and then pointed a sharp fingernail at him and growled. "I *should* sever our ties altogether... choose another." She narrowed her eyes, but he did not mirror her callous expression. Derek's look was of worry and fear, and I could wholly imagine the anxiety of being cut off from one's Sire. Of being *abandoned*.

"But," she continued with a huff of discontent, "a Sire's responsibilities are immense and the years have weathered my patience. I do not wish to seek out another so soon." Her golden eyes flickered with light. "I must admit that my hasty decision to take you was not all in vain."

Derek was taken aback by her comment. He opened his mouth to reply, but Ve'tani raised a flattened hand.

"Silence!" she said. "Or I may change my mind."

"What is to be done?" Matthaya asked.

She cracked a coy smile, as if she were pleased with herself for the plan she had conjured. She glanced over at me, then at Matthaya, and lastly, at Derek.

"Bite him," she said flatly.

"What!?" Derek's eyes widened. "Why? Why would that—"

Ve'tani shot a fierce glare his way. "You asked for my help," she roared, "and I have provided it. Now take my advice, or I *will* leave you behind." She flicked a hand at Matthaya and me. "Bite him! Both of you! You have wasted enough of my time."

There was immense doubt in Matthaya's eyes and his feelings bled into my consciousness.

"How do we know you're not trying to trick us into

killing him for you?" Matthaya asked. I had just thought the same thing.

She scoffed. "If I had wanted him dead, I would have done it myself. Why would I waste my time waiting for *you* to do it?"

The disdain in her expression convinced me she spoke the truth.

I wrapped a hand around Matthaya's. "She's been around much longer than any of us. Maybe it will work."

"Do *you* believe her?" Matthaya asked Derek directly.

"I don't know if I'm in a position not to." He staggered nearer. "I poisoned you." He looked me in the eye before slowly taking to his knees. "Do what you will in return." He lowered his head and lifted both arms up and out to the sides until the insides of his wrists faced the sky. "Even if it kills me."

"Why both of us?" I asked Ve'tani.

"Because Matthaya is *your* Sire," she replied. "And our venom strains are too alike to cancel each other out completely. But, by adding your own, which has been altered by this new era, it may be enough to neutralize his grasp on your mind. In lay terms: he bit you, you both bite him, things go back to the way they were." She shrugged. "With any luck."

I looked at the faded forking lines inside my wrist.

His venom would stay in me forever.

I had no choice but to listen to her. Even if Derek chose not to access my mind ever again, his consciousness would always be there, haunting me from afar like a secondary Sire. I couldn't let his existence interfere with my own.

Ve'tani didn't sound completely confident that this would work, though. That bothered me.

Matthaya reached for one of Derek's wrists.

But it *had* to work.

I hesitated, staring at Matthaya for some kind of assurance that what we were about to do was the right thing. He didn't have to say a word for me to sense his feelings. They convinced me that it was *our only chance*—that we had to try.

I reached for Derek's other wrist and his arm tensed in my grasp. "You're *sure* it won't… hurt him?" I glared back at Ve'tani and her fierce golden eyes gazed back at me, an air of smugness to her expression.

"Oh, it *will* hurt, but pain is better than death." She smirked. "Is it not?"

What kind of creature found joy in someone else's suffering? Ve'tani really was a monster.

"It's the price he must pay," Matthaya said. He was fairly confident that this would work, despite whatever side effects occurred.

I lifted Derek's hand higher and then bent down until

my face was within inches of his wrist. Anxiety surged through me as I neared his skin, and I felt the intense urge to pull away, my instincts compelling me *not* to do what I intended.

Matthaya came down toward his other wrist and a glint of green light flitted through his eyes as his jaws eased open. He, too, had to shake off the uneasiness.

We weren't supposed to bite our own kind. It was ingrained in us to avoid it and to fear it.

I inched closer to the darkened, red-purple veins beneath Derek's skin and my vision began to shift, changing colors as light in my eyes ignited. I couldn't control the rage billowing inside me—a vivid, feral desire to retreat from the foreign, undesirable blood of another vampire.

But I knew I had to do it. I needed to free myself from his control.

My mouth opened and my fangs closed in on the fragile skin of his wrists. As I sunk my teeth into his veins, he cringed and let out a low, forceful huff, falling forward. Our grasps on him tightened as a potent, bitter taste hit my mouth and my jaw clamped down. Heat pressed through me—my venom propelling into his bloodstream.

A strained wheezing sound resounded from his throat as he threw his head back and his face wrinkled with agony.

Matthaya and I released him abruptly, in tandem.

He tumbled forward, scrambling to stop himself from hitting the ground. A trail of dark blood oozed from his wounds onto the grass and he hunched over, shaking.

I wiped my face with the back of my forearm and a splash of burgundy colored my skin. The acidic substance burned my mouth severely and I spat out blood and coughed. The taste lingered on my tongue.

Matthaya was more graceful with his disgust and wiped his lips subtly with the cuff of his sleeve; he was strong enough to endure the unpleasantness.

A deep churning throbbed in my stomach and I felt the urge to vomit rising up my esophagus. I clenched my fists tightly, fighting back the unusual sensation.

Derek hadn't been so successful; he plummeted toward the ground, coughing hard as his fingers dug into the earth, tearing into soil and grass. He heaved and a splash of black-red blood spattered the ground.

"I'm sorry." The words came out beneath my breath and I took a step toward him. Matthaya reached out to stop me, a shake of his head advising me against it.

I stood there and watched as Derek strained to compose himself, another wave of gut-wrenching pain welling in his throat.

It was difficult to watch, and even more difficult to fight back the urge to comfort him in some way.

A few moments passed and he sat back on his heels

and wiped his face with the back of his hand. With great difficulty, he came to his feet, avoiding eye contact with us.

"Derek?" I took a step closer. "Are you... okay?"

He didn't respond.

I looked at Ve'tani, who was watching him intently, and then asked, "Is he—?"

"Yes," Derek finally replied, turning only partway to face me. He trembled and clenched his teeth as another wave of pain or discomfort washed over him, and he turned his face away. He sucked in a shuddering breath and bit down again, stifling a groan.

I approached him swiftly and pressed a hand to his shoulder. "Derek?"

Matthaya's anxiety spiked as he thought to pull me away, but he remained where he was in observance.

"Derek, please look at me." I squeezed my fingers against his arm. He refused to look me in the eye.

"I'm sorry," I whispered.

He faced me, gawking in disbelief. "Why are *you* sorry?" He coughed again.

There was blood, his own, on the crease of his lips. I raised a hand to catch it before it dripped down his chin. He froze as I slicked it from his face and then wiped my fingers on my pant leg.

His rich brown eyes stared into mine and his brow

crinkled, but I could not feel his emotions or presence inside my mind anymore.

It must have worked.

"I just..." I started, unsure of how to reply. "I didn't want you to suffer at my expense. Not again."

"I deserved it for all the things I did to you." His posture softened and sorrow shadowed his eyes. "And I would never call the time I spent with you before I was taken... 'suffering'."

His words stunned me. Was he not bitter about all that had happened? Was he not bitter about my wanting to say 'no' to his proposal?

"But I do have one question," he said. "Please. I'll never be able to ask it again."

He lifted a hand, looking as though he might stroke it across my cheek, but then stopped himself.

Matthaya growled from behind me.

Please. Trust me. I tried to calm him in my mind.

He let up, but only a little.

"Tell me the truth, though," Derek added. "It's all I ask."

I nodded in agreement.

"Did you *ever* love me?"

The truth? What was the truth? How could I even answer that question?

A gust of clarity swept through my mind and it felt

more spacious—Matthaya had backed out of my sub-conscious thoughts. I looked back at him briefly. He had withdrawn several steps and was allowing me the chance to search for my answer privately.

I felt grateful to him for it.

The truth...

That night—the one that seemed eons away now—when Derek had thrown caution aside, taken me into his arms, and kissed me—was a night I would never forget. The warmth of his body close to my own, and the pas-sionate touch that stole my sorrows away and fought back the fears lingering in my heart. At that moment, a surge of emotion and need grew in me and I had consid-ered sharing a life with the man who'd handed me a broken heart to mend, trusting and believing that I somehow had that power.

Hearing this wouldn't put an end to the pain or bring closure to him. It wouldn't quell the regrets or set him free from the tangled web of mistakes I'd made.

But, I digress...

Did I ever love him?

"No," I replied, looking him straight in the eye.

I was thankful the vampire disease repressed a flinch.

Thankful that tears would never well in my eyes, nor would a shudder resound in my breath.

Thankful that vampirism allowed me to lie.

"I see." Derek looked away, nodding slowly, as if he'd known the answer all along.

"I apologize for using you when I needed someone," I added. "You rescued me from the awful home life—you were my lifeline. You opened up your heart and you gave me a chance. For that, I will always be grateful."

Always...

I wanted to reach out to him, but I abstained.

"Matthaya and I are bound by more than this lifetime."

"He left you..." Derek uttered, a hint of bitterness still coloring his words.

"Yes, he did. And I had nowhere else to turn. I'm sorry, Derek. I'm so sorry. I never meant to hurt you. Please believe me."

He remained silent and I swallowed hard, waiting—*hoping*—he would respond.

I waited, feeling uneasy as I watched him stand there with his arms crossed and his mouth sealed in contemplation.

He wouldn't say anything else to me.

I looked back. Though I could see neither of them, I knew Ve'tani and Matthaya lurked nearby. Then I looked back at Derek, whose broad shoulders and strong back suddenly slumped, and whose once proud, rigid form had bent and softened with defeat.

"Derek?"

"I do."

"You do what?"

"I believe you." He shrugged. "That's the part that sucks—the part that cuts the deepest." He shook his head, his face rose, and our eyes met for a fleeting moment. "I believe everything you've told me, and that's why it hurts so goddamn much." He scowled.

Derek was a brave man. He was strong and confident, but it was clear that my words had broken him, stripped him down to the bare bones of his soul.

I never wanted to relive the appalling dreams he'd forced upon me, but in them—behind that vengeful façade—was a semblance of a man who had loved me.

The pale-skinned creature standing before me was a shell of that man.

Past Derek's silhouette was a spark of vivid amber light in the distance—Ve'tani's eyes. Derek lifted his head and turned toward them as if he'd been summoned. Then he returned his gaze to me.

I mouthed the word, "goodbye," knowing it might be the last time I'd ever see them.

"Take care of the shop for me," he whispered, and then turned his back on me.

As Derek walked away and his form slipped further into obscurity within the distant shadows of the wooded area behind the slum, Matthaya neared my side.

When the others were far enough from us that I could no longer feel their presences, I said quietly, "He's trapped with her forever."

"They'll be fine," he replied, taking my hand and entwining his fingers with mine.

"What if she *abandons* him?" There were fates worse than death, even for those of us who have seemingly escaped its grasp.

"She won't," he replied, shaking his head. "She's a vain, sentimental old fool. Ve'tani does not make mistakes, nor does she admit it when she does. Even Sires need companionship. You and I both know she is still wounded from my parting, though she hides it behind malice. She needs Derek as much as he needs her."

He was right. I knew he was right.

Would I ever see Derek again?

Should I even be thinking about that?

He had tortured me. He had burrowed into my mind and torn me apart shred by shred until he had fractured my soul.

He broke me, left me fearing the one man I thought I could never fear.

And yet, I forgave him; I even pitied him.

Derek had loved me, and in his warped, tormented state, he could find no other way to tear the bandage from the wound I'd left on his heart than with revenge.

I should have hated *him* for it, but the fact of the matter was I hated *myself.*

I hated myself for what I'd turned him into—a monster inadvertently forged by a series of naïve decisions.

I glanced down at the inside of my wrist—at the small, dark spots left by his venomous bite—and they reminded me of the large scar I'd once seen along the side of Derek's ribs. It was a mark from his first brush with death at the hands of another, and I remember being fascinated the first time he told me its back story.

We all carry scars from our pasts.

We are all haunted by something or... someone. Aren't we?

"You did the right thing," Matthaya said, drawing my attention away from my rampant thoughts.

"Did I?"

"You told him the truth."

"I told him what he needed to hear."

25

MATTHAYA

THERE WAS not much to speak of on our return home. Kathera ruminated over the evening's events, and I let her because there was nothing more I could do. She had said her part and he had said his and they had gone their separate ways peacefully.

At least, that was my understanding. I did not listen in on their parting conversation. It was not my place to do so.

"Matthaya!" Kathera called to me from the kitchen.

"Yes?" I entered to find her typing fervently on her phone.

"The doctor, she's already here."

Already?

She had told us her plans to stop by on the...

I had forgotten what day it was.

Today.

"She said she's at the hotel waiting for directions." Kathera looked down at her shirt and bloodstained hands. "I'm not ready for this right now. I need to—"

"No." I put a hand onto her shoulder.

"What?" Kathera looked up at me.

"Not tonight. Tell the doctor something urgent came up, and that we will make arrangements to meet her tomorrow. I have already promised to settle all her expenses."

"Are you sure?"

The hunger was brewing inside me already, and the stress of the night's events had made it come about more quickly. I could feel it rising in Kathera, as well, though she didn't seem to have noticed yet.

"We have had a very long, taxing evening. You and I are in no condition to have company."

"Don't you want to know what she has to say?"

"Of course, I do," I replied. "But I also want to do so with a quieted mind and a body unhindered by bloodlust." I stared at her. "Wouldn't you agree?"

Disappointed but understanding of my point, Kathera nodded and then began texting the doctor to request she delay our meeting until tomorrow evening.

It was for the doctor's own good, really.

ℬ ℭ

Daylight came and went, and the following evening blew in like a storm, barely allowing us enough time to make arrangements for the company.

"She should be here soon," Kathera said, peering out the front window. Her anxiety and anticipation put me on edge, but I knew she was looking forward to speaking with Dr. Henson.

Sounds of a car engine neared and then the car shifted into neutral momentarily. A car door opened and closed and then the vehicle drove off.

I knew the proper way to greet the doctor would be to meet her at the door, but—

"Good evening, Doctor," Kathera said, standing in the entryway with the front door propped open.

My wife had already taken that liberty.

I returned to the kitchen to boil a kettle of water on the stove.

"How was the trip over?" she continued.

"It was fine, thank you for asking," the doctor replied. Her voice was warm, silvery, and highlighted with a French accent. "Kathera, was it? Oh, I hope I didn't

236

botch that. Did I say it correctly?"

"Yes. Perfectly."

"What a wonderfully unique name. It's lovely to finally meet you," the doctor went on. I didn't need to be in the same room to know she had set a small briefcase down; it clacked against the wood flooring.

"My hands are very cold, I apologize," Kathera noted. I assumed she was shaking hands with the doctor.

"Oh, my, they are. My mother's are the same way." The doctor chuckled. "Is your husband here?"

"Yes. He's in the kitchen."

A strange, brief flash of panic went through Kathera, but it wasn't strong enough for me to worry. She was likely excited or anxious about the meeting.

I heard their footsteps approach, to which I turned and tried to present a friendly smile.

"This is Matthaya," Kathera introduced me. "Matthaya, this is Dr. Eleanor Henson."

"Call me Eleanor," she chimed.

"A pleasure to meet you," I replied, shaking her hand.

"Cold hands all around," she said with a chortle. "I apologize for my silliness. Still fighting jetlag, you know." She looked down at my hand and narrowed her eyes just before releasing me.

"This cufflink is immaculate... 18th, no, 19th century?

May I ask where you acquired such a gorgeous replica?"

They were not replicas.

"I would prefer you didn't," I said.

"Oh." She cut a glance at me and then released my hand. "I'm sorry for being rude. I get excited about random things."

"No need to apologize," Kathera interjected. "We're very grateful for your knowledge." She gestured toward the stove. "Would you like any tea or coffee before you sit down?"

We did not typically have such things in our home, but since we knew we would have company, we attempted to make our place look lived in, or at the very least, *human*.

"Tea is fine, thank you," she answered. "No sugar or milk."

Good, because we had neither.

Her request for tea, though, reminded me of Prince Eddy, and how he would partake in a cup with milk after spiriting away to his quarters to read a secret letter from his beloved, Hélène.

A seed of sadness sprouted in me as I remembered him again. But there was no time for that now. This was supposed to be an uplifting meeting.

Kathera moved past me and reached into the cupboard for a brand new mug and then opened a sealed box of black tea that was sitting on the counter.

"I'll take care of it," she said.

She poured boiling water over the teabag. Steam rose and danced above the cup as she placed it atop a saucer and handed it to the doctor.

"May I show you to the living room?" I asked.

We entered the next room where Kathera and I sat side-by-side on a sofa and the doctor sat across from us on a plush chair with a nearby end table to support her drink.

"I see you're wearing it now," she said, nodding toward my right hand. "May I please take a closer look?"

I slid the ring off my finger, scooted to the edge of the seat, and then leaned across the coffee table to hand it to her.

"Thank you." She cupped it in her hands carefully and looked it over with immense enthusiasm. "This is remarkable. The craftsmanship. The etchings." She turned it to the side and brought it closer to her eyes. "The rune in the dragon's tail... I believe it's UI or Uillenn. It's part of Ogham—a very old medieval alphabet used in early Irish."

"What does it mean?" I asked.

"Well, you can see that the line of the tail curls inward, like the golden spiral, if it were made of squared corners. The Uillenn is perceived to represent a honeysuckle or woodbine plant. But the use of the curve in this design—aside from being a letter in the old alphabet—clearly symbolizes something more, seeing how it was cleverly crafted into the dragon's anatomy. Typically, when it's used for personal adornments, UI symbolizes discovery or a twisting labyrinth. The search for self and purpose through the winding turns of fate."

She revealed her phone. "Do you mind if I take a few pictures of it myself?"

"Go ahead." I wasn't ecstatic about it, but what harm would be done?

She held the ring under the light of the lamp beside her and began snapping photos with her phone.

"Did your wife tell you about my thesis?"

I glanced over at Kathera and shrugged. "Only briefly."

Eleanor turned the ring over and took several more photos before returning it to me.

I slid it onto my finger, relieved to have it back.

"My thesis was on the British occupation during the 17th century and its effects on the Irish Chieftains of the South Eastern region. Now, I don't know if you've read my most recent book or not, but let me tell you some of the things I discovered with my research."

Picking up on anticipation and anxiousness rising in me, Kathera reached over and set her hand atop mine.

"Well, the Irish tried to get out from under the thumb

of British rule for years, and in 1594, some of the most powerful clans came together to try to fight back in what was known as the Nine Years' War. It lasted until 1603, when the clans finally surrendered to the Stuart King, James I, but that's not the important part." She reached for her tea, took a sip, and then set the mug back down. "Chieftains O'Neill and O'Donnell fought alongside the Spanish in an attempt to push back against the English government. But it is my belief that they were not the only ones involved in this fight—that not all British were on board with the whole taking-over-Ireland thing." Eleanor shifted in her seat and leaned toward us, lowering her voice as if she were about to tell us a secret. "I have always theorized that there were, in fact, English sympathizers in the country—defectors, of sorts, who had mingled with the native people and whose opinions had been swayed in their favor as a result.

"These defectors were assimilated into the Irish clans, with one of them having a leader of full English blood at their helm. I had read bits and pieces of literature hinting at this secret organization and its raven-haired Chieftain, but all references were completely devoid of names."

"Are you suggesting that the British group of sympathizers were ghosts?" I asked.

"No. No. I'm saying they hid their identities in order

to protect their families and, possibly, their relatives back home. But I'm getting off track here. What I really want to say is that I found evidence of this group, but even though there were no names attached, there was a very distinct symbol used to identify members—a dragon. But, not just any dragon! A three-horned dragon with a rune curled in its tail."

Her suggestions were outlandish, but...

"You are meant for great things," my mother had told me, the day I was released to my fate as an indentured servant. The ring was the only thing she had given me to remember my father by. The memories were hazy, but I clung to them with every shred of my being.

"How do you know all this?" I asked. "Were other rings found?"

"That's just it," she continued. "Before you contacted me, no one has ever been able to find a ring or signet of any kind. But..." She pulled up a photograph on her phone and turned the screen toward me. "We did find a wax seal on a letter written to the other Chieftains from the defector clan's leader. Now, if you turned your ring just to the side. Take a look."

The design embossed in the wax seal looked uncannily familiar. I spun my ring around my finger and studied the engravings on the sides. It was possible the ring was used to make the mark.

"Your ring may be the most important clue in my search to prove the existence of the British defector clan."

"I'm sorry to interrupt," Kathera started, "but if this is all he has left of his family, are you saying that his fa—" She stopped herself. "Are you suggesting he may be a descendant of the leader of that clan?"

"Not necessarily, but it is possible," Eleanor went on. "It's also possible the ring was stolen, gifted as a token of loyalty, or... if we really want to go there... removed from the Chieftain's dead body in battle. But, yes, if you want to think of it that way. You could be related."

"But you haven't been able to discover the identity of the clan leader, right?" I asked. "The man who supposedly possessed this dragon emblem?"

"Unfortunately, not. But the mere existence of the ring could be enough to prove my theory and that might gain the interest of other historians who could do additional digging." She laughed to herself in disbelief. "I mean, I could rewrite history with this knowledge."

"I wish to remain anonymous during your investigation," I said. "As I have stated prior, this ring is all that remains of my past."

"Don't worry," Kathera said. "The doctor and I have already discussed the confidentiality of this."

"Oh, yes." Eleanor straightened up and reached for her tea again. "Your identity is safe. I've taken more than enough photos to assist me. You've done every-thing you could. I'm only sorry I don't have more concrete details for you at this time. The British Chieftain did an excellent job covering his tracks. Even if I never dis-cover his name, at least I can prove he existed."

That wasn't exactly what I had hoped to hear.

Eleanor sipped her tea and then cupped it in her lap.

"One more thing," she added. "Would you show me the painting we discussed, as well?"

"Give me a moment," I said, standing from the sofa. I entered the next room and retrieved Kathryn's por-trait. Normally I'd have had it displayed on the fireplace mantel, but I had removed it so that I could bring it out in my own time.

"There she is," Eleanor said, standing as I walked back into the room. A smile of warmth and awe curled her lips. "Could you set it there?" she asked, pointing to the large coffee table between us.

She reached down to the floor and rummaged through a side pocket in her briefcase, retrieving a pair of white fabric gloves.

I gazed at her inquisitively.

"I always carry these. You just never know what you may find, and I don't want to get dirt or oil on your beauti-ful painting."

She lifted it up from the table to take a closer look.

"The paint is in remarkable condition. Very little varnish discoloring. Very few cracks in the oil. Did you have it restored?"

"No."

"Then this is in some of the best shape I've ever seen for a painting of this age. It's a shame the artist died before he could create a legacy. He was very talented, indeed."

"When did the artist die?" I asked.

"Not long after he made this, actually. He did one other like it, a few for other elite members of society, and then disappeared for weeks before being found dead in a field just outside Paris."

"That's terrible," Kathera said.

"Did you say there was *another* like it?" I asked. "Of the same subject? Of Kathryn?"

"Yes, actually. There is one more painting of Kathryn Shallon. It was done post-mortem—her mother had it commissioned as a keepsake. It doesn't have nearly the amount of vibrancy and... *life* that yours does, however. I have a photo of it on my phone if you'd like to—"

"No."

"I understand." Her eyes shifted and she appeared to be hesitating. "Actually, that's something I wanted to speak to you about. I managed to trace the girl's lineage and learned that she has living relatives."

If my heart had still pulsed, it may have skipped a

beat.

"How!? She... I thought she was an only child."

"She was," Eleanor added. "But after the poor thing committed suicide, her parents had a second child—another girl. Her name was Margery and she went on to marry an English soldier by the name of Edward Hughes. They had many children, though, and the lines of the tree have tangled up quite a bit over the years, but I've managed to piece together most of it."

Something about the tone of her voice and the rapid pitter-patter of her nervous heart made me uneasy. She was suspiciously knowledgeable about two very different, but integral, parts of *my* life.

"Why does her lineage concern you so much?" I asked. "I thought you were only concerned with proving your theory on the British defectors?"

"I-I am." She put the painting down onto the table and then tugged off the fingers of her gloves one by one. "This is definitely authentic and also highly sought after. I've been in contact with someone who is *very* interested in purchasing this. They are willing to pay you a fair price if—"

"I have no interest in selling it." A quiet growl vibrated in my throat.

"Would you consider allowing someone to replicate it? A professional reproduction done by a specialist, on canvas. I'm sure the interested party would compensate you for the time and inconv—"

"No." I stood and retrieved Kathryn's painting. "I cannot—will not—allow it to leave my residence. You will have to tell your *client* to look elsewhere."

It annoyed me that she would propose such a thing. I was under the impression that she was a famed historian, not an art dealer.

I set Kathryn's painting back on the mantel.

"That painting means a lot to him," Kathera said softly.

"I see that now," the doctor replied. "I apologize for being uncouth."

I turned to face her. She set her tea and saucer on the side table and checked her phone for the time. Her heartbeat was racing still.

"Well, it is getting quite late," she said. "I don't want to be a nuisance so I'll call a ride and head back to my hotel now."

"I'll take care of that for you," Kathera said, pulling out her phone and launching an app. "You're welcome to wait here, meanwhile."

"Thank you, Kathera," she said, smiling gratefully. "I hope the information I provided was enough." She looked back at me.

"It was insightful," I replied, attempting to force a

smile. "Thank you for coming all the way down here to speak with me and my wife about your findings. I do hope the photographs help you prove your theory. If there's anything else I can do..."

"Thank you." She stood and picked her briefcase up from the floor. "Thank you for the tea, also."

"Your driver should be here soon," Kathera announced, showing the confirmation screen on her phone to the doctor. "Don't worry about the fare. We'll take care of it."

"You two have been so very kind to me."

"You have been kind to us, too," Kathera added. "You've done so much research."

"I only wish I had more information about the ring, or a name to place with it, but the Dragon Clan didn't leave anything behind."

"Dragon Clan?" The title piqued my interest.

The doctor sighed. "Just me filling in the blanks again." She grinned and shrugged. "It's not really an official name. I mainly use it in my notes for reference."

I reached for the doctor's teacup and saucer.

"Thank you," she said.

I took them to the kitchen and set them on the counter.

There was something strange about Eleanor, but I couldn't place it. An odd sensation had flitted through Kathera, too, as soon as she had entered our home. I had thought it was anticipation, but now it seemed like something else. Nothing about her was particularly extraordinary, but there was no mistaking the strange air of her presence.

A few minutes later, I heard a car pull into the driveway.

"It was nice meeting you," I said to the doctor, as I returned to the living room.

"You, too," she replied. "I'll be staying in town for a few more days to do some sightseeing. If either of you wish to join me, please don't hesitate to call or text." She reached out to put her fingertips on Kathera's forearm. "Please keep in touch, dear." Eleanor's smile was bittersweet.

26

KATHERA

WHEN DR. Eleanor pressed her fingers against me, a buzz of energy flitted over my skin like an electrical shock. And each time our eyes met, I gained a sense of comfort from it.

I walked her to our front door and then waited in the doorway for her to get into her ride and drive away. Sadness, and even a sense of loss, crept into my heart as the taillights vanished into the night. Why did saying goodbye to a near stranger feel so awful?

"She was an interesting woman," Matthaya said, walking with me back into the main room.

"Yes."

The unusual feeling churning inside me didn't cease, not even now that she had left.

"You don't..." I started, looking over at Kathryn's painting. I juggled the ridiculous suggestion a bit before saying it out loud. "You don't think *she* was the one who wanted to buy the painting, do you?"

Matthaya's eyes widened and he gazed back at me as if he, too, had suddenly come to the same realization.

"I heard her heart beat faster when she spoke of it," he said. "Almost as if she was afraid to ask, but compelled to."

"And I..." I tried to put the feeling into words. "I felt something when she arrived. I don't know how to describe it, but it was as if she were familiar to me. As if we are... connected in some way."

"That would explain why she has done so much research on Kathryn's painting and her family lineage. Kathryn may have been a baron's daughter, but her stature did not automatically make her a significant historical figure. I've done enough research on her, myself, to have learned that. I could not sense the same thing you did, but it pleases me, to know Kathryn has living relatives."

"I don't think she could tell, though, do you?"

"Tell what?"

"That we're... different."

"I don't believe so. If anything, she was blinded by excitement over our antiquities."

"Maybe we could allow her to have just one copy made of Kathryn's portrait," I suggested delicately. "It may be as significant to her as it is to you, just for a different reason. You don't know how long she's been trying to find it, and she doesn't have eternity like you did."

"You're right," he surprised me in reply. "I'll consider it. I know she doesn't have all the time in the world, but she will be here for another week. Perhaps you can bring it up later if you decide to meet with her again."

His thoughtful words brought a smile to my heart. I was hoping to stay in contact with Eleanor, seeing that she and I shared a special link.

"Thank you. I would like that, and it is my hope that I can."

I approached him and took his hands. "So, how do you feel now that you know a little more about who you are?"

"It's not definitive, by any means," he replied.

"I believe it," I said confidently, squeezing his hand. "Think about it. The 'raven-haired British Chieftain' who tried to free Ireland and who sympathized with its people. You said it yourself that your mother believed you were meant for great things. She probably wanted you to carry on his legacy somehow, even after he died in battle."

"That would mean that I am half English." His brow furrowed. "All these years, I believed I was—"

"Maybe you and Kathryn had more in common than you realized." I brushed my thumb over the emerald ring and smiled at him. "You told me yourself that you'd even convinced Prince Eddy to accept the position of Viceroy of Ireland in an effort to promote much of the same cause."

Matthaya seemed stunned by my ability to string all the details together.

"You really believe the doctor's theory, then?" he asked.

"I think she's on to something," I replied. "I believe it all makes sense, and I absolutely believe that this is who you are. What did she call them? The Dragon Clan." I rested my hands on his shoulders, knowing that hidden behind his strong frame was a magnificent pair of wings. "I think it perfectly fits who you have become."

27
KATHERA

AN EMAIL from Kieran arrived with details on the tattoo sought by the man inquiring about the apprenticeship earlier. Still at home, I opened it, expecting to see reference images about the design he wanted, but instead found a portfolio of his personal works, followed by a small sub-section about the tattoo. At the top of the email, Kieran implored me to take a look at the man's work *before* making the final decision to say no to his inquiry.

Knowing how interested Kieran was in the idea provoked me to consider what it might be like to have an apprentice artist in the shop. It didn't mean that I *had* to teach them tattooing—not unless they had wanted to learn—but the thought of having a new artist to collaborate with intrigued me.

When I opened the attachments, I was taken aback. His creature work was intricate, dark, and dramatic; it showed a high level of skill and dedication. I could also see that my style had been a heavy inspiration for him by the way his line work flowed across the page and the dynamic poses used.

When I was a young nobody with a crazy dream of being a tattoo artist, Derek gave me a chance, even though I didn't have a thread of job experience under my belt.

Maybe it was time for me to pay it forward. Derek had asked me to take care of the place, and I'm sure if he saw this guy's work, he would have given him a shot.

I picked up my phone and dialed the number listed in the email.

He answered quickly.

"Is this Brian?" I asked.

"Yes."

"Hi, it's Kathera from Restless Ink. How are you doing tonight?"

"I-I'm doing great. Thanks." His voice wavered nervously. "Uh, how are you?"

"I'm fine. I got your message about the tattoo you're

wanting, but I'm actually calling about the portfolio you attached. I'm looking over it right now."

He went silent.

"How long have you been drawing?"

"My whole life, I think. Since I was maybe 6 or 7? I don't remember, but I know I got into trouble at school when I was little because I was scribbling on everything. My mom got pissed."

He sounded young, maybe in his late teens, but I didn't want to make assumptions.

"So why do you want to work with me?" I asked. "And what do you hope to learn?"

"Well, I've been self-taught all my life, but I've been using your work as inspiration since I was in middle school."

Looking over the vivid and ferocious wolves and anthropomorphic beings he'd drawn, I could clearly see my influence, even though the subject matter was very different.

"I'm just having trouble finding my personal style," he continued. "I was hoping you could help me better my techniques and composition. That way, I could concentrate on developing my own style."

"Your work's very good," I commented. "I will admit, I had no plans to bring anyone else onto my team, but I think I could teach you some skills that would help you grow."

I heard him gasp.

"You sound like a smart guy who knows what he wants to accomplish, and you persevered even after I said no. Your portfolio has definitely changed my perception, so thank you for having the courage to send that to me."

"You're welcome. Thank *you* for your kind words about my art. Th-that really does mean a lot to me."

"Could you come by tomorrow afternoon? Maybe after 1 p.m. so we can discuss the details of your apprenticeship. Does that work for you?"

He went silent.

"Brian?"

"Yeah. Sorry. I'm just really looking forward to meeting you in person and, hopefully working with you. Thank you. Thank you so much, Kathera. Yes, I'll be there for sure, tomorrow, 1 p.m. sharp."

"No need to apologize. Oh, and while we're on the subject, let me just say that your name, Brian Azure, is a great fit for this industry. It's distinct. I like it."

"Thanks. I'm glad you think so." I could hear a smile in his voice.

"See you tomorrow. Have a good night, Brian." I ended the call.

I went back to the email he'd sent me and swiped through the different scans of his drawings. His werewolf was impeccable, and I could easily see it being something one of my clients might request, had they seen it. He'd drawn several urban mash-ups, too. Superhero-esque characters with thick lineart and dramatic poses. There were also a few skulls mixed in that were better than some I'd seen at full-scale shops downtown.

Looking through his fresh, unique work—clearly *inspired* by my own—made me think more about my aspirations.

It had been a very long time since I had sat down and drawn something truly new and different. Something that came from my heart and not my nightmares. Something that had a life of its own.

It had been a very long time since I was truly inspired.

Since I had become a vampire, fewer things inspired me. It was as if the world had been cloaked in a transparent mist, giving everything a dull overcast.

Thinking back, the tattoo that launched my career was of a dragon—a tribal dragon I'd designed for Derek. It was my original idea, but heavily inspired by Derek's work. It shaped me into the artist I am today, even though my own style eventually took over and I started to create very different things later on.

I went to my art room and retrieved my sketchpad, a pen, and a pencil from my desk. Maybe I could rekindle some of that feeling by starting something new.

"Matthaya?" I called to him from the living room.

He was in the bedroom reading, trying to get his mind off the craziness of this week and the doctor's visit.

"Yes?" He entered the room and glanced at my sketchpad.

I looked him in the eye for a few moments, taking in the majestic, captivating green I had very much fallen in love with.

"I'd like to try something new," I said, clasping my sketchpad close to my chest. "Would you... help me?"

"With your art?" He tilted his head.

"Yes. I have an idea and... I need a model." I tried to smile optimistically.

"And you want that to be me?"

"Well..." I looked him over briefly, trying to piece together my request in a way that would not make him uncomfortable. I must have lingered on the thought too strongly, as he sensed it.

"My wings?" he asked, a tremor of discomfort flushing through his mind. "Why would you wish to draw me like that? My wings are what make me the awful thing that I am. They—"

"Make you what you are, but they don't make you a monster," I corrected him. "Your wings are beautiful, and they have protected me several times already. They are majestic and special."

I felt disgust and shame roiling through his thoughts over the wings he had grown to loathe. In his eyes, they solidified the fact that he was a creature of the night—a vampire in all usual definitions of the word, and beyond.

But to me, they symbolized hope and change— evolution and moving forward.

"They make you unique, and I admire them."

"You... do?" Matthaya lifted his head and a barely noticeable grin tugged the edge of his lips.

"Yes."

He stared at me for several moments, contemplating whether or not to comply.

Before I could offer reassurance or pose the question differently, he unbuttoned his coat and slid it down off his arms. He draped it gingerly over the back of the sofa and then began to unbutton his dress shirt.

After the last button came undone, he slipped the shirt off and set it near his coat. I put my sketchpad down and approached him. He tensed up slightly, at first; he had always been uncomfortable with the visible scars of his past.

I lifted a hand to trace the top of his shoulder and gently stroke a line down his arm, smiling at him in admiration and appreciation. I circled him briefly, taking in the details of the large jagged scars streaking his back and coiling over his shoulder blades and around his ribcage, toward his chest. The scars were tragic reminders of the pain he'd endured for his love of Kathryn—and the terrible thrashing dealt by her vengeful father. The lines of his wings were cleverly hidden beneath those scars, the bones sunken flush against his skin and into the shallow but specialized indentations in his ribcage.

The webbing of his wings melded perfectly with the pale skin of his back, and the only tells of their existence were the small curved claws comfortably hidden and barely visible at the base of his neck, below his hairline.

There was a cracking sound. The two sharp hooked claws behind his neck lifted up and then the segmented arm bones of the wings began to rise, stretching and unfolding from his back and straight behind him several feet.

The skin of the wings was flaccid, at first, crinkled and rubbery. Within seconds, blood from his body flushed into the veins, making the skin stretch until it was taut and smooth like leather.

The wings pulled in until they were only part-way open and Matthaya asked, "Will this do?"

"Yes. Thank you," I replied.

I felt a sense of calm come over him now, as if he had finally allowed my feelings of fascination and appreciation to quiet his discomforts and doubts.

Before I could start drawing, I had to analyze the structure carefully. I had seen them several times in the past, but he'd never really allowed me to understand how they worked—the astonishing mechanics and anatomy that allowed him to keep them secret for so many centuries.

The main arm bone of each wing had been segmented in three distinct places, which allowed the end of the wing to fold inward, onto itself, not unlike a compact umbrella.

I touched the skin of his back just below his shoulder blades, at the starting joint, and traced my fingers down his skin. There was a subtle indentation in his back where his ribs had become slightly concave in order to allow the wings to settle flush near his spine.

The gray flesh with pink undertones was velvety, with a texture close to the rest of his skin, but firmer and more durable. He stretched his wings out to the sides and the joints moved smoothly, like a dancer's arms, gliding with perfect fluidity and control, capable of a surprising amount of motion and coordination.

I stood before him, facing him again. He brought one wing around, with great precision, and used the hooked claw at the top of the joint to swipe my bangs to the side of my brow. It was a gentle, deft movement that mirrored the sweep of a finger.

His other wing curled forward and cupped me from behind, putting gentle pressure on my back to coax me closer, pulling me into what I could only describe as an angelic embrace.

He grasped onto my hands and tipped his face to press his forehead to mine. I closed my eyes.

"Thank you for accepting me as I am," he said. Our noses touched.

He released me, and his wings withdrew slowly, folding close to his back, the claws resting at the base of his scalp.

I reached for my sketchbook and took a seat on the couch while Matthaya retrieved a nearby bar stool and sat down in front of me. It was a tight fit in our living room, but his wings could open to a comfortable distance.

The pencil kissed the paper and I began making gentle strokes to put down the basic outline of the shape. I reinforced the lines of his bones with firm pressure, and then carefully added the sharp claw to crown each wing. The exact placements of the joints were tricky to portray, but with some determination (and several adjustments) I captured their nuances with some justice. After the main shapes were down, I lined them with thick, black ink.

A smile began to grow upon my lips and joy within my heart, as I gazed upon him in all his beauty.

As a vampire, much of my creative fire had turned to embers. Still, a glow sparked to life in me when I looked at him—a radiant cinder pulsating with life from beneath the ashes.

My husband may have been the son of a great man who left behind a fierce, but mysterious, legacy in an effort to help the Irish break free of British rule. Although his father lost the fight in the end, his fearless spirit lived on in my husband—a man with the strength of an entire cavalry and the lifeblood of centuries flowing through his veins. If ever there were one, *he* was a true representation of that Dragon Clan—forged by the ages and compelled to bring two peoples together.

Matthaya faced his future with grace, authority, and the white-hot fire of courage in his blood. That fire ignited the fuse that would revive my creative spirit and resurrect my calling.

Inspired and unafraid, Restless Ink flowed through my veins once more.

A Note From The Author

It is my belief that earnest fiction is derived from truth; therefore, I do my best to present some new or interesting knowledge to my readers. With every novel written, I learn more about my characters and I grow as a person.

The amalgam that is Matthaya's past is forged from many historical facts. When I wrote the original *Dark Diary*, I knew even then that he had befriended a young duke in the 19th century, and that the duke had died of pneumonia at a young age. When I began my research on the subject for *Grave Burden*, Prince Eddy's story resonated with me, and I absolutely knew he was the duke in question.

Readers often ask how I create and shape my characters, but I believe my characters shape me. Their life journeys take me to places I have never been, driving me as an artist. In the case of this novel, it was both with great pleasure and a heavy heart that I learned the captivating story of a forgotten prince.

The Duke of Clarence and Avondale, Prince Albert Victor Christian Edward of Wales—Eddy—lived a fleeting life, fraught with obstacles. Since he had been born prematurely and had difficulties in school, it was theorized that Prince Eddy suffered a learning disorder, or ongoing illness, along with possible complications from absence seizures (brief, sudden lapses of consciousness, or "zoning out"). These afflictions made life for the young prince difficult and put a strain on his family and the public, igniting a series of rumors on behalf of the media in an effort to push him further from the throne.

He enrolled in Trinity College, Cambridge, where he did not thrive as his family had hoped, and was also sent on numerous tours of India, Scotland, and various countries in the British Empire. In an effort to "toughen up" the future king, he was instated into the Prince of Wale's Own cavalry, where he was promoted to captain.

None of these endeavors seemed to alter his nature, and after his romance with Princess Hélène was shot down by numerous high-ranking individuals, Eddy fell into a deep depressive state, even threatening to denounce the throne.

Though I could not find proof of the correlation, there *is* scientific evidence that people can, in fact, suffer and die from a broken heart—a condition known as takotsubo cardiomyopathy, in which the heart balloons into a Japanese pot-like shape. It generally lasts a few weeks but can cause severe problems, or death, in those of already compromised health.

It would seem, even in death, Eddy simply cannot rest.

In 1962, long after his failed love affair with Princess Hélène and decades after his death, allegations that he was Jack the Ripper were initially brought up in print.

To support these ideas, writers made spiteful claims that the prince's early demise had been plotted or even faked in an effort to remove him from succession. All of this couldn't have been further from the truth.

Eddy was stationed at Balmoral Castle, Scotland, at the time of the Whitechapel district, London, murders in 1888. Still, the outlandish rumors persisted in the media and several novels, even making it into films such as *Murder by Decree* (1971) and *The Ripper* (1997), to name only a few. These depictions blatantly ignore the fact that Prince Eddy was nowhere near Whitechapel during the murders, in an effort to capitalize on the life of a man who could not defend his reputation.

Prince Eddy's life and likeness were later spun into other fictional worlds in titles such as *Elseworlds* by DC Comics, multiple Sherlock Holmes mysteries, and even portrayed as a vampire in Michael Romkey's *I, Vampire*.

It is my hope that Matthaya's story has allowed you a less fantastical glimpse into the life of the tragic prince Eddy and his heart-breaking tale of forbidden love.

To view an astonishing, intricate memorial for the prince, commissioned by his family, I recommend you search the internet for his tomb designed by Alfred Gilbert.

Although not completed until the early 1900s, the art and sculpture are breathtaking.

The following pages feature memorial engravings extracted from original 1892 printings from my personal library. I acquired the original carte de visite (CDV, French: visiting card) albumen photograph of Prince Eddy (also shown), but the date of creation is not precisely known. It is my estimation that it was taken between 1880-1890, as Prince Eddy seems to have a more youthful appearance than in later depictions. CDVs were small, business-card-like photographs (usually 2.125" x 3.5" plus a slightly larger mounting frame) patented in Paris by photographer André Adolphe Eugène Disdéri in 1854. Since they could be replicated in larger quantities, they were often collected and traded. By 1870, they were commonly supplanted by cabinet cards, which were larger, mounted albumen prints.

If you're unfamiliar with albumen and the process used to make photographs with it, I highly suggest looking up videos online. Coating a sheet of paper with a concoction of salt and egg whites, and then later adding silver nitrate allowed early photographers to capture and preserve glimpses of our past. It is my hope that you enjoyed this peek!

CDV enlarged to show detail

The Last Portrait Of The Late Duke Of Clarence By
Professor H. Herkomer Is Presented With This Number.
January 23, 1892

A
DOUBLE NUMBER
OF THE
GRAPHIC
* IN * MEMORIAM *
PRICE, One Shilling.

Office: 190, STRAND

THE LATE DUKE OF CLARENCE AS AN OFFICER OF THE
10TH HUSSARS.

Thank you for reading!

If you enjoyed this story, please support the author's
writing journey by posting a review on Amazon
or social media. Share your thoughts with friends,
other readers, and book clubs.

More from P. Anastasia:

Fates Aflame & Fates Awoken
Adventure that will lift your spirits and romance to warm your heart

Magical journeys await you in this clean epic sci-fi fantasy. With newfound powers at hand and a dragon by her side, Lt. Hawksford, star student of a prestigious military academy, must face trial by fire.

Exile of the Sky God
"An effortlessly grand fantasy..." — Kirkus Reviews.

An adaptation of the lore behind the Sky God, Horus, one of the most powerful gods in ancient history. Embark on a mythical expedition of self discovery with extraordinary revelations.

Fluorescence: The Complete Tetralogy
An infectious saga read across the world

Alice was a normal teenager until a dying race of aliens chose her to preserve their bioluminescent DNA. Fluorescence evolves from quiet beginnings into a gripping tale exploring the real-life dangers faced while harboring a volatile secret.

The series includes:
Book 1: Fire Starter
Book 2: Contagious
Book 3: Fallout
Book 4: Lost Souls

P. ANASTASIA'S fresh take on storytelling resonates with darkness, charm, and passion—the embodiment of her unique writing style.

Ensnared by the craft in childhood, she attempted her first book at age eleven. While working toward her college degree, she wrote news and editorial columns for two campus newspapers. After graduating with a degree in communications and spending a year studying abroad in Kofu, Japan, she followed her heart to her publishing aspirations. She currently resides in the beautiful, green state of Kentucky with her husband and her ever-inspiring fur-babies. On the side, she serves as a professional voice talent for radio, television, and audio books.

P. Anastasia is the author of nine novels: *Exile of the Sky God,* the *Fluorescence* series, *Fates Aflame, Fates Awoken,* and *Dark Diary.*